METEORITES

Dedicated to and in memory of Gordon Dixon.

Daniel.

I try to breathe, to stay calm, but it gets harder every second. Not to stay calm, but to breathe. In fact, the harder it gets to breathe, the easier it gets to be calm.

The dying side of me realises how weird it is that I'm becoming calm, because I really, really shouldn't be.

But that's me, or at least that *was* me.

The world outside me, seems a distant place. Gravity seems to have no tie on me anymore. Some of her old teachings come back, how strong but also how weak gravity is. That the gravitational field strength of this planet is 10…Newtons, I think ….no, newtons per kilograms…and…and….I could never escape gravity, even if I left the atmosphere of this planet.

But gravity becomes weaker. The further away from Earth I go, the weaker it will be.

All I know right know, is that despite by body's weakening state, my mind and perhaps my soul, if it exists, is strong enough to beat gravity. And there's only one thing holding me back to Earth.

Seren.

She's holding my hand, like she can never let go. In her soft voice, she talks about Jake's ambitions to study Meteorology at the University of London, even though that means he will have to move away from Buckinghamshire.

She says that tomorrow, we can go and see that movie at the cinema that we both wanted to see.

Well, that's Seren for you. Always trying to deny the truth. Always trying to achieve the impossible, and never able to let go.

My thoughts come quickly, rapidly. Somehow I hold them all in my fading mind.

Seren, I'm so sorry for all the fights we had, even though we always made it up.

There is a black oblivion, a dense fog inside my own thoughts. As I try to think, the oblivion becomes stronger, until I know it is more powerful, more forceful than me.

Seren. Oh God, Seren. I'm sorry.... for all the.....pain I'm about to cause you.

Don't forget me, but don't hold on to me.

Be happy, in whatever you do.

I wish I could say that to her face, rather than think it, but I've got to hope, that I can think it loud enough so that she can hear it. And I know that's stupid, but it's the most important thought I've ever had. She has to hear it, because I'm asking her to do something I know she can't do.

I try to breathe, small rasping breaths, try to let Seren have her way for a few more minutes, but it's too hard now. I have no control. The black oblivion has cut off any new thoughts, and extended throughout my body.

And I don't just want to give up my world just like that, but... I've never felt so calm, and still. I can barely hear the monitor that shows I'm alive just for one more second.

But I can still feel Seren's hand holding me down with her, but I know I'm almost gone because it's lighter than it's ever been. My last tie to Earth is gradually going.

Did I tell Seren I loved her enough? Did I ever say that to my parents? Do they even know I'm here?

Seren will know to give them my love, she always knows what to do.

What will it be like going? Will it hurt?

I can't feel Seren anymore, but I know she'll still be holding on. She will until she can be convinced that the end is over.

Goodbye.... Seren I....I love you.

I'm still. I'm calm. I'm almost free.

Gravity fades. There is darkness prickled with pin points of light.

My mind curls around into a whirlpool decreasing in size.

My sensation of Earth is almost gone, when I hear a small voice, sounding as if it is trying to hold back falling stars.

"Daniel I love you... I can't....cannot ever express how....sorry I am....for causing this".

Her voice sounds so final, so lost, so…it scares what little of me is left.

No! Seren! Don't! This was not your fault!

I want to scream that out, yell it out, bring it out in any way I can… but I can't. I can't!

I hear my heart monitor suddenly give out a long beep, and stop.

Then I'm gone.

(1) Seren.

I once told Daniel my name meant 'star' in Welsh. He said that was ironic because he had always wanted to see a meteorite- a shooting star, but he would settle for me, because I could become 'shooting' angry, and I would get 'fiery'. I then decided to put my science knowledge to 'good' use, and explained that a shooting star was *not* a mete*orite,* but a mete*or.* He laughed, and called it the same thing. At that point, I did turn into a bit of Meteorite and gave Daniel a science lesson on comets, meteors and meteorites. I don't think he appreciated it - or understood it.

Mum says it's okay, and good that I think about those things. It'll help. But how is it helping, when it causes me more pain, than I would feel before?

I don't want to think about it. It's only been weeks, since the worst day, and everybody's already wanting me to move on. I know going on the treadmill 24/7 is not what they meant. But it's the only time that I can let myself *think.* Or not think. Because when I'm on the treadmill, I have to think about running, and only half my brain can focus on what happened. And if I go fast enough, I can either stop myself thinking about it at all, or I run past the point of pain, and I can't feel anything. And that's what I want for a few seconds. To feel nothing. To feel numb.

I'm going too fast, I know it's dangerous, but it's not working today, I want to feel nothing, I don't want to feel anything. I want to banish my thoughts, by going fast enough, so I have to focus on moving with the treadmill, moving with the flow. Moving on.

"SEREN!" comes a voice, belonging to my younger sister, surprising me, forcing me out of my thoughts. I jump, lose my stride. The fast moving treadmill takes me along with it, depositing me over the edge, banging my knee against the cold metal. I wince, then look up to find my six year old sister staring at me, her eyes wide.

I want to yell out a whole chain of expletives, but as my tell - tell sister is right there, I confine myself to a "Holy, bloody crap".

Lily gasps "You said TWO bad words".

"Since when was 'Holy' a bad word?" I retort.

My sarcasm is lost on Lily, it seems.

"Not that one. You know C-R-A-P, and 'B-L-O-O-D-Y" she says, spelling it out.

"Bloody is not a bad word, when your annoying T-W-A-T of a sister has made your leg bloody" I reply.

"STOP SAYING IT!!" She cries out.

Oh...my ...god! Two weeks ago, Daniel and I would have annoyed her and teased her, but right now...

"Oh shut up Lily!" I snap.

My sister never knows when to let it go.

"There's no need to be mean about it, Seren".

"Yeah, whatever, Lils", knowing perfectly well that she hates that nickname.

She carries on.

"And you were going so fast! It's dangerous! I think I should tell Mummy...."

Something inside of me snaps at that point.

"Yeah, alright, Lily, you do that. OH, I know, why don't I tell 'Mummy' what an annoying, IRRITATING, BABYISH LITLE PRAT YOU ARE!!!"

Lily stares at me for a few seconds, then her lower lip trembles, and she runs out of my room.

I groan. I'll definitely get into trouble for this later. Mum will probably ground me. What she doesn't seem to understand that I actually like being grounded, so I can stay in my room, and don't have to look at the pitying looks my parents and my two siblings seem to relish giving me.

I examine my knee in further detail. Strange. A tiny cut can give out so much blood. You think you're badly injured, then you clean away the red scarlet, and find a small cut that looks like you made a big fuss over nothing.

You listen to him when he says that he doesn't think it's serious, that blood looks worse than it actually is. You listen, when he says that it'll just take a few stitches, but you already know, but can't admit that he's lying, because you will always listen, and don't let him know that you know that truth. You hold his hand in yours, and you say goodbye to Daniel, as he dies, with you watching.

(2) Daniel.

I remember once in a lesson, we had to think about what colours represented human emotions, like anger, pain, and peace. Obviously, everyone chose white as peace. I thought red, was anger and pain. My reasons were pretty narrow minded, like red was pain, because it was the colour of blood.

But I think I got it wrong. Because, I'm surrounded by White, but it's not peace. It's pain, leaving your family and the girl you love behind. It's anger, knowing that the girl you love, blames herself for what happened, and is back on Earth, where a week ago, you were alive.

It's strange, and hard to describe. Somehow I know I stand at a crossroad. In front of me is a way to peace, of letting go. It means letting go of life completely. Letting go. Accepting your death. I don't know what lies beyond, what religion is right, but it's free. But I don't know if I can let go yet. Something that is more than my own thoughts, something a little stronger than mental, a little weaker than physical holds me back.

Behind me, is a way back. A way of being with life, though you aren't alive yourself. A way of blending with your old life, though you can't live it. A way of coming back to Earth.

I can't be free just yet. I'm coming back to Earth. I'm coming back to Seren. And she should give herself more credit. I did understand the meteorite lesson- she's a good teacher.

(3) Seren.

I can’t sleep. I can't sleep even though I'm tired enough. I've tried all of the methods they say work. You know, stay calm, shut eyes, and think of something nice. But I still feel as awake as I did before.

It's an odd feeling. I feel tired but wide awake. Also numb, but that's nothing to do with it. It's not the reason I can't sleep.

I want to sleep. Maybe that's the problem. I can't get enough of the irony of that. Most people my age don't want to sleep or go to bed. They complain about unfair bedtimes, and really awful getting up times. But most people my age, don't have to deal with their boyfriend dying suddenly.

I shut my eyes, to try and block out the thoughts that start swimming around my mind. If I don't think about it, it might get better.

In my dream, Daniel is next to me. Its summer, a few months ago we’re curled up on a picnic rug in my back garden. It's hot, and I can Lily scream and giggle as she plays with the garden sprinkler. My older brother Jake is joining in, and squirting her with a water gun. Between us is a creased copy of ‘The History of Britain’ which Daniel gave me for a present. We're supposed to be reading but Daniel seems more preoccupied with catching stray strands of my loose auburn hair.

The sun slants across him, showing off the blonde highlights in his brown hair. In the light, his brown, chocolate eyes shine even more than they usually do.

It's calm, despite the screams of my brother and sister. Daniel looks at me like he usually does, and tucks a loose strand behind my ear. His hand lingers softly against my cheek. He laughs softly and gently. He turns back to the book, and begins to read out the dialogue.

The next morning, I wake early, but don't open my eyes, wanting to keep him with me, a little longer. But I know it's only a dream. It's too hazy, to perfect. A perfect day that will never happen again. A small tranquil moment that was disturbed by the click of a camera, and the laugh of your brother as your sister turns the sprinkler on you.

But then that small memory turns into a sea of scarlet red, and I have to open my eyes to stop the pain from spreading.

The light of day hurts as my eyes adjust. There is small ray of light coming from a small gap in my bedroom blind. I turn my head, and look at the clock. The red digits read 7:30.

I used to wake up around ten, on a weekend. It used to annoy me, because I would waste part of the day. Now all I want to do is sleep, but that seems barred to me.

I listen out. No one's up yet. I don't know if that's a good or bad thing. I decide to grab a book, as I'm not going to go back to sleep.

So I turn my light on, and change my attention to the stack of books, balancing preciously on my bedside table. I reach my hand out to grab the nearest one, not really caring what it is. But as I'm not looking at what I'm doing, instead of grabbing it, I knock it off the table.

Groaning, I look in the space between my bed, and table, to see if I can grab it, without getting out of bed.

Instead of one book, lying there, there is two. I'm not surprised, as I have so many books, and my room looks like a meteorite hit it at the best of times.

Luckily for me, it's quite easy to grab both books. The first book is 'The Hunger games'. I - *we* wanted to see that movie.

I place it back on the table, and look at the second book in my hands. My hands begin to shake, and my breath comes in short gasps. Because the book I find in my hands, it's 'History of Britain'.

That's just a little bit of a *freaky coincidence.*

I haven't looked at that book for a while.

I was reading it, but then a week ago...I forgot about it.

Too many memories I didn't want to think about.

Then I notice something sticking out of the book. Probably a piece of paper marking my last place. I wonder what I was reading. Because I let my curiosity get the better of me, I open the book.

My question's answered. Winston Churchill, but that's not what takes my attention. Because marking my place is a photo. But not just any photo, a photo of the day I just dreamed about.

A dream. Two books. A photo. Something tells me, this isn't, it can't... just be a coincidence.

(4)

I used to enjoy just looking at the stars. Literally, I would just grab a rug and go lie in the garden. Kind of startled my brother the first time - I was lying so still, he thought someone had killed me. My brother can be quite imaginative – and a bit morbid sometimes. Somehow, I got it in my head that I needed to see a meteor - I can't even explain why, but for some weird reason I decided to watch a meteor shower. Unfortunately, seeing as I lived in Britain, this was easier said than actually done.

Every time, it was always never to be seen. It was either cloudy or raining - it was the worst of Britain's luck-but the best of Britain's predictability.

I can't explain why I loved the stars so much, and I don't think I will ever think of a reason why

But does there really need to be one?

Everyone always tries to explain everything, they forget to enjoy. Because part of human nature needs answers, need explanations, needs logic and reasoning. This part of human nature is more dominant, needs more attention.

Maybe some people have it more than others, but explanations seem to always be needed.

But if look more closely, you might be able to uncover another part of your nature, that simply craves enjoyment. That is content to ignore all logic, all reason, and just revel in the present. This side of you can enjoy and wonder, without thinking why this wonder happened.

It can allow you to lie back in your small garden, and just gaze hazily with eyes that never will cease to be amazed and wonder.

It stops you from thinking, who, what, where, how, and just allows you to enjoy a simple thing, perhaps one of life's most simplest, but maybe Life's most important for that very reason.

But it's a small fleeting sensation, being able to block out a part of your nature. So it's never long, before the real, more shown side of humanity, breaks through your reverie.

I often get bored, there's not much to do here, so sometimes I look at the stars, but it's not quite the same, I suppose the wonder left, when I said goodnight. So, the other times, I observe. They still fascinate me but because of what they represent.

What if each star was a small figment of humanity? Clearly, I know what they really are, but it doesn't stop my imagination.

What if each star was a life, back on Earth? I know that a lot of people feel stars are small fragments of spirits that left the Earth, and joined the expanse, of what is only known when it is your turn to join.

I also know that a lot of other people feel that a shooting star falls, when a star lets go of gravity, allows itself to be free, it's when someone on earth is letting themselves let go of their ties to life, and becoming weightless, unbound.

So with that logic, each star could represent a life. So many stars out there, some yet to be discovered, some yet to be created. So many lives out there, some not heard of, some yet to be born.

Some stars shine brighter than others, they dominate the sky. Some lives dominate the others, they are the ones most sought out, more heard of. But if we didn't have so many stars, all shining, would we have such a bright night?

From a distance, it could seem that every star is the same, but if you dare to look a bit closer, then you might be able to tell the differences.

Nothing, anything or everything is the same. But I still observe, and I still wonder. Not to be clique, but nothing is the same - though that doesn't mean that nothing can be similar.

As we are all of a species, as we are all of humanity, there should be some similarities, but though all my observations, I am yet to find one. And it doesn't make sense. There are similarities in our nature, but not similarities in our personality.

We might meet someone who we feel is similar to ourselves. But is this because we are too scared to look deeper into ourselves? Look deeper into our nature, because we are scared of what we might find?

Sometimes we might just be carrying on with life, doing what we usually do, when a small voice inside of us, stirs, voicing an opinion you never realised you had. Could that be another part of human nature, that you keep subconsciously keep imprisoned, scared to let it loose?

Is that the real human nature, crushed beneath pressure of the nature that you might have craved to suit? Are we all scared or worried to show the real, real side of us?

And it still doesn't make sense. How can one person, so different from another be part of the same species? How can one person, the evilest on the planet, be part of the same race of the gentlest child that graced the Earth?

And there's that side of human nature peaking though again. The side that needs logic and explanations. Maybe it's also the reason, why it's hard to find peace?

(5) Seren.

My imagination could be quite vivid sometimes. Or most of the time. Actually, if you really got to know me, you would then find, it's really all the time. I just hardly show that side of me. Hardly anyone would really want to hear about what weird thoughts I came up with. I also don't really want anyone finding out how screwed my brain actually is.

So, I had a lot of thoughts going through my head, when I found what I found. Most of them, weren't that rational and contained a lot of strong language.

I have no idea how long I stared at that photo. My hand started to shake a little bit. Oh course, my first thought was *Daniel*, then my imagination kicked in, along with unladylike language.

My breathing got a bit rapid at this point. *How... why... How...* I even admit that one of my thoughts was *Daniel's alive.* Another one was *Spirits.*

My thoughts were a jumble of my imagination that were getting me into too much of a state to comprehend.

After a while, my sense of rationality returned, and I was able to sort through the thoughts my mind had left behind.

But only one was rational: *You simply knocked over the books, and marked your place. You had a dream, nothing more, and nothing less. You just let your imagination take control.*

My hand shakes, as I place the book back on the table. On second thoughts, I get out of bed, grab both books and put them in a drawer I hardly open.

I don't know what to do with the photo though. I don't want to tear it up, so I place it in the drawer as well. I slam it slightly harder than necessary.

There's no point in believing in miracles, because they don't happen. There is no point believing in spirits, and ghosts and the supernatural, because they just can't be real - it's not rational.

I ignore the tiny thoughts in the back in my head, *you used to believe in spirits, it can't have been a coincidence,* and one more, *who says the world has to be rational?*

But believing in spirits, is not going to help me anymore than not believing in them is.

Right now, I can't bring myself to believe in them, because it's not going to do any good-I'll just end up, in small broken pieces that I'll have to piece together.

Because it would lead me to hope, and the last time I hoped for something, a miracle, it didn't do anything.

I grab another book, from the small stack and try to get engrossed in it, before my mind starts thinking. Before I start crying, because crying never did or never does anyone any good.

One good thing you can say about Victorian literature, is that it stops you from thinking. So, after struggling with a few chapters of 'The Hounds of The Baskervilles', I put Sherlock Holmes down, and listen out.

My bedroom is above the kitchen and sitting room, so I can easily hear if someone is up. For some weird reason, I don't like being the only one awake and the first person out of bed.

Luckily for me, I can hear someone, draw back a chair and start walking. I can then hear some water flowing, then someone waking back to the chair. Considering this person is sitting in the kitchen, rather than the nice sofas in the sitting room, it's probably my brother Jake. He's got his A Levels soon, and taking it very seriously. Literally, when he's revising, he sits at the kitchen table, if no one is up, because: 1. His room is below a very noisy water tank, and next to a bedroom, belonging to an six year old, who talks to imaginary friends, and 2: It's not as comfortable as his own desk, and chair, meaning it won't distract him, forcing him to concentrate more. *Um, right.*

Honestly, I don't think it works like that. You focus on your revision, because you know how important it is. But to his credit, it is the Easter holidays, and most people his age would be playing on their X-boxes, and not bothering to actually do it. And if it works for him...

So, I decide it's time to get out of bed. I'm too lazy to actually stand up. So I shuffle my body down my bed (so my head won't bump onto my table), and roll sideways, off the mattress. My duvet supports me, and stops me from falling on to the floor, stopping the impact, and then it gives way, allowing me to land on the floor, giving a smaller shock.

I smile wryly. It seems that what my life has turned into. Slow and supported, then falling fast.

I pick myself off the floor, and grab my dressing gown. I take care to be quiet - I don't want to wake anyone up.

I open my bedroom door slowly, as it's quite creaky, and tiptoe across the landing to the stairs. Once downstairs, I turn left into the kitchen.

Yep. My suspicions were correct. Jake sits at the table, with about 10 million text books in front of him.

"Hey Seren" he says, without looking up.

I frown "How did you know it was me?"

Jake finally looks up, with a cocky grin on his face. (Adopting a weird, posh, Victorian accent) "You know my methods, - My deductions were correct".

I raise my eyebrows ."Have you nicked one of my Sherlock books?"

He's silent for a minute "....Maybe".

I roll my eyes. "When you're finished, just put it back where you found it".

"No problem, sis".

I turn around to grab the carton of Juice and a cup. "So how did you know it was me?"

"No one else wakes up earlier than you… nowadays…and because it's the Easter holidays. Except maybe Lily, but she isn't as quiet as you."

I inwardly smile. "Well… you're up".

"Yeah, but you woke up earlier".

I think for a second, then face him, turning around slowly.

"How did you know I was awake though?"

Jake doesn't say anything for a good few seconds. The tension increases. A weird feeling for us both.

Just when it seems too much, he looks down "I heard you....cry out".

I stare at him, slightly confused. "But... I didn't cry out. I had a dream, but.... I woke up... I..."

He looks at me with concern. "Seren, I think you must have yelled out, without realising it".

"That's... possible?"

He shrugs. "I guess - I mean, you're just gone through something...quite traumatic".

I try a shaky smile "The power of the mind huh?"

Jake looks at me oddly, blinks and nods once, accepting the fact that I don't want to talk about 'The traumatic incident'.

"So, which Sherlock book did you grab then?" I randomly say, in a bid to change the subject.

"Um, A Study in Scarlet".

"Oh, I like that one!" I say brightly, in a failed attempt to hide any false notes.

Jake, also willing to change the subject, rolls his eyes dramatically "You like anything to do with literature- you even read Les Miserables".

I pretend to give him an evil look "That book is brilliant".

"No, the movie with Amanda Seyfried is brilliant!"

Now, it's time for me to roll my eyes "You like anything to do with Amanda Seyfried - you even sat through Mamma Mia!"

"Who's 'Manda Sti-fry?" says a sleepy voice belonging to Lily, who stands in the doorway of the kitchen.

Jake and I exchange a quick glance. "How long have you been standing there Lily?" Jake askes with a frown.

She shrugs, almost looking like a teenager. "I don't know - I heard you talk about something called Lee's Miserable - why is Lee Miserable?"

Jake and I exchange another glance, but a more relaxed one this time.

Jake chuckles. "Because he had to read an awful book, about a French Revolution – I mean, come on Seren, it's not even about THE French Revolution!"

I look down at the now-empty orange juice carton in my hand. For once, my throw is *perfect.*

(6) Daniel.

When memories hit you, it can bring more pain than can ever be imagined. Forget all of the battle scenes, and executions seen in 'Lord of the Rings' or 'Game of thrones' (I'm still not over the Red Wedding), the power of your own imagination and mind is the strongest. And you have two choices: you either close your mind off to the wave of memories, or you let them hit you, and bow down under the pain...but when you straighten up again, it can bring every emotion you have or have never felt:

"Are you sure about this?" asks Seren nervously, as we walk down the street, her hand loosely tied with mine.

I grin. Seeing as Seren hasn't pulled away her hand, she really doesn't mind, she's just trying to give the impression that she is the more responsible, mature one of us. An argument I won't bother to deny. But still, Seren is inwardly enjoying this, I can tell by the easy smile she is attempting to hide, and the little sparkle in her eyes.

"Absolutely. Don't worry, we're not doing anything that will get us into *serious* trouble...."

She looks at me sceptically "Okay then, what kind of trouble will it get us into... and what actually are we doing? You haven't said anything other than 'we need to be careful'".

I pretend to think about that. “Well, I don’t think they can place charges on two teenagers for sneaking into a hospital to visit a friend”.

Seren stops walking, and her hand tightens around mine.

“That’s what we’re doing?! We’re going to see Ally?” she starts to yell in excitement, which grows more voluminous by my nodding.

She laughs, but then her smile drops.

“But… she’s in intensive care. It’s only family allowed in”.

I look at her.

“That’s why we have to be careful”.

She looks blankly at me for a few seconds, then registers my meaning and her smile grows wider, and brighter, and stronger.

It freezes for a second, as she suddenly realises something.

“Wait there” she says to me, and runs into one of the small corner shops lining the pavement.

10 minutes later, she comes out holding a plastic shopping bag.

At my curious gaze, she opens it up, allowing me to look inside.

It is completely full of strawberry milkshakes - the expensive luxury kind, made with real, organic strawberries, and all that.

"Ally asked me to sneak some in, if I could" she explains.

Oh yeah, I remember now - they're Ally's favourite drink. She's not really supposed to have them that often, so it's easy to forget that.

But not for Seren.

I stare at her for a little bit. Seren's face begins to look confused.

Without even thinking, I lean over, and kiss her on her cheek.

She blushes first, red roses illuminating her cheeks.

Then she smiles, and quicker than the speed of light, I see her eyes suddenly shine.

I take her free hand again, and we walk towards the Hospital, with that casual, sort of swinging, slow steady speed that only teenagers who know they are alive have.

A few minutes later, Seren and I are crouched behind the door of the Intensive Care Unit. The nurse on the entry desk hasn't looked in our direction *once*. This actually might be quite easy!

"Right, you definitely know which room she's in?"

Seren nods. "Just texted her".

She passes on her phone to me, with the text displayed.

I give it a courtesy glance, noting the numbers and directions that Ally has thoughtfully provided, along with a request to explain what prison is like, if we get caught.

"Okay".

I stand up.

"I'm going to distract the nurse. As soon as she is paying attention to me, run for it! I'll join you in a few minutes".

She nods.

"Right. But how are you planning on distracting her?"

I grin at her.

"Watch me".

After pretending to beg the nurse to 'just let me see Alexa for just one moment-I'll be so quick! Please! We're practically cousins!', I turn away, and pretend to wipe away a tear, and I see Seren sneak past into the unit.

I inwardly grin, and turn back to the nurse, and sigh.

"So there's absolutely nothing you can do?"

The nurse shakes her head.

"No, I'm so sorry".

I nod sadly.

"I am too......OH MY GOD, IS THAT MAN HAVING A SEIZURE!"

I point to the waiting room. The nurse turns, and I make a run for it.

Once in the unit, I slow down to a walk that I make confident. If I act, like I belong here, most people will think I do.

And it works. By the time I get to room 221BBS, I have passed over 5 doctors, and a few nurses, and no one has even looked in my direction. The door has a little window. Before I go in, I peer through it.

Part of me tells me 'that I'm making sure it's Ally's room', but the smaller part of me knows the real truth.

A small skinny girl sits cross-legged on the bed. She wears loose clothing, and a hat, even though she's indoors. She looks like she is trying to hide herself within a new portrait of herself.

She's holding a strawberry milkshake (courtesy of Seren Ambern), but is waving her hands around so much as she talks, it's a good thing she hasn't opened it yet.

On a chair next to her, is Seren. The girls are laughing about something, which has made Seren blush red - making Ally laugh even more. I smile, but also frown, guessing who the topic of the conservation is. Ally makes a comment, and Seren catches my eye, mid laugh, and waves me in the room. And before she caught my eye, her own were filled with stars, that brightened when she saw me.

(7) Seren.

I groan, and change the channel yet again. How come, when you're not watching television, the best programmes are always on, but when you actually do turn it on, you have to skip about a million and one channels until you find a program that you will watch, even if it is a Disney movie, or some cheesy crap you last watched when you were 10. And then, someone will come into the room, laugh and roll their eyes at whatever you're watching and 'tactfully' suggest you do something else. That suggestion will cross your mind, and you might start thinking about something else you could do. You might even do it. But more times than not, you turn the TV on, because you are bored, and when your mind just wants a distraction.

So, this is why I'm sitting on the sofa, next to Lily, aimlessly flicking though channels, not really paying much attention to Lily's requests. "I LIKE that program", "Turn that one on!"

After about a billion channels, Lily, quite frustrated, snatches the remote of me, changes the channel to some animated movie, and sits on it. She then cringes away, expecting me to mercilessly tickle her for the remote.

She frowns, as she realizes, that I'm not going too, and I really do not care. "Seren?"

I shake my head "Anything's better that what's on the other billion channels".

She looks confused for a second. "Okay".

She turns her attention to the television and we don't speak again for another hour.

Watching Lily watch TV can be quite funny sometimes. She has a habit of blocking everyone and everything out, and creates her own little world, that just contains herself and whatever show she is watching. Because she's in her own little world, she doesn't bother containing her emotions. So while I stare at the TV blankly, my sister giggles, chuckles and laughs at whatever crazy things characters in Disney movies do.

Lily and I used to watch TV all the time together. And, oddly, her emotions would make me laugh as well, because I found it funny that she had so much emotion, to waste on cartoons and movies, how the smallest thing would make her happy, a feeling I always wanted to make her feel.

But now, I just don't...care. She's sitting next to me, still laughing, but I don't feel any emotion. It doesn't annoy me, and it doesn't make me laugh. I'm just blank.

I swing my legs, laughing as the momentum drags me higher and higher. I grab the chains tighter, knowing if mum could see me, she would begin freaking out. Jake swings next to me, trying to get higher, so he can win the fight.

Soon he gives up, I hear his feet scrap against the gravel, and clinking of chains as Jake gets off. I also hear him mutter about him, a mature 12 year old, having to take his nine year old sister to the park, as dad wants them out of the house, and then having to go on the swings.

I wait for my swing to slow down to a stop, then hop off. Jake waits for me, leaning against the frame, mobile out. He looks up at me. "Dad wants us home now".

I grin.

"Is Mum back?!"

Jake grins back and shrugs. "I don't know - He didn't say - C'mon, let's go.

We walk back home, quickly.

As we get to our street, we see that the car is parked in our drive. We grin again, and run into the house.

In the sitting room, Mum, looking exhausted, sits, holding a small bundle that is either our baby brother or sister.

Next to her, sits our neighbour, Nicole.

They smile at us, but motion for us to be quiet. Mum beckons us over, and I look over to the opposite sofa, where Nicole's son Daniel sits.

He smiles at me. That surprises me, because he's never shown much interest in me, but then again, I rarely see him, coz, even though he lives across the street, he doesn't really socialize, but...

"Seren?" I slowly come back to myself, to find Lily is shaking me, and Jake is standing next to me, looking at me weirdly, with a mix of concern, and panic.

Lily hasn't quite realized to stop, so continues to shake me violently, but I don't have the voice to stop her. And when, I try to speak, all that comes out is deep breaths. Jake puts his hand on Lily's shoulder and gently pushes her off. He then kneels down to me.

"Seren, what happened?"

But I still can't speak. Then, suddenly I feel water trickling down my face, and my body is racked with tremors. Jake looks really panicked now. Lily starts yelling:

"IS SHE DYING??!!!!"

And as she talks, my subconscious tries to grab me back down. Jake's voice seems distant and far away, but I can feel his hands on my shoulders, trying to calm me down, as well as trying to reassure Lily.

I need to get out of here NOW, cos all that's here reminds me of the memory, and it will drag me back down under. The sitting room I sit in, Lily, Jake.

I remember shaking him off, shaking myself free. But I don't remember how I ended up running down the street, with Jake in pursuit. I don't even know where I'm going or what I'm doing. It makes me laugh, which makes me choke. How can I be laughing? How could Lily be laughing? There's nothing to laugh about anymore!

It's raining, but the droplets are just indifferent to me. They bounce off me, and I barely notice. Nothing can stop me. I want to run, and run, and run. And If I have to stop, I have to think. And if I have to think, it'll be about things I can't think about. I don't care about the pain in my legs and lungs, I welcome it - it's a pain that's bearable.

Jake's behind me, begging me to stop. But how can he understand? I can't, I just can't. Then he yells out my name.

Recognition begins to flow through my mind, in what must have been less than a second. I'm on a road, and there's a speeding car coming towards me. And I don't know, if it's my messed up state, but I swear that I can hear another familiar voice calling. My shattered mind starts to come back, but I still can't comprehend.

Until a hand grabs my arm, and pulls me back on to the cold safety of sanity - or reality, and pavement. Jake runs up, his face a mask of pure horror. I gasp out, and my mind is mine again, not overrun by demons of memory.

Jake grabs me, by both arms and I can see his body shaking. "You *idiot,* what the hell were you doing!?"

"I don't know, Jake, I really don't know". I stutter out.

He looks at me, assesses I'm not lying, then his St John's training pops into place.

"You're probably now in shock - I think you had a panic attack". Jake also tries to lighten the mood "you *may* have Hypothermia - C'mon, let's go home". Before, we do go, he turns to face the man that pulled me out of the way. He rolls his eyes at him.

"Wow, when I said come over, I didn't think you would have to save my little sister! Thanks for doing that!"

I look at him properly, and recognise him as one of Jake's new friends, from a St John Ambulance group and revision session.

He nods in my direction, and smiles a bit awkwardly "Don't mention it".

For my benefit, he adds "I'm guessing you're Seren - I'm Nathan.

(8)

'What we leave behind is not what is engraved in stone monuments but what is woven into the lives of others'.

I think I would have liked Pericles, if I had been born in Ancient Greece. Shame nowadays, we don't have politicians whose words will live for centuries.

I was 18, when I had to leave, but I left behind no stone monuments, and was barely woven into other lives.

My life was small, and unlived. You never really know what you really miss, until it's too late. When I lay, slipping away. My mind started to fill with the things I had achieved. But then thoughts of what I could have done flooded, and took over.

I was going to be a violinist, I was going to marry, have three children. I would write in my space time. I would try to compose. It didn't matter what I had done, it wasn't enough. I never drank alcohol, I never went to Australia.

Scaling down, I could have lived until I had 80 years, I got 18. Thinking that way, I got a fraction of what I could have been, what I could have done.

But now, here, I start to think. Actually think. I got about a quarter of what I could have been. Looking at it that way, makes it sound so negative, so bland.

But look at it another way: The live you did have, the life you lived beats the cold facts of Maths.

I had 18 years, I had my 18 years. I lived my 18 years.

*I learned how to speak four languages. I read. I earnt As and A*s in my GSCEs.*

I danced with the man I loved under starlit skies.

Maths doesn't rule everything.

(9) Seren

I sit on the sofa, changed into dry clothes, but also with a blanket draped around me, because I still cannot stop shivering. Nathan sits across from me, and I'm actually glad Lily's still here, because Nathan and I have no idea what to say to each other. Lily chats mindlessly, and manages to dilute the awkwardness.

Jake enters with a tray full of hot chocolates and offers them around. Before he sits down, he chucks over to me a Cadbury Dairy Milk.

"I don't need that, Jake" I say, chucking it back.

"Like hell you don't". Jake responds, walks over and places it in my lap.
"The sugar will do you good. The last thing we need is *that* happening again!" he adds drily.

I glare at him. "*That* didn't happen because I was low on sugar!"

Jake looks at me infuriatingly calmly.

"I'm not saying that. But sugar will help deal with shock".

I shake my head. "I don't need it".

Jake raises an eyebrow "You *never* turn down chocolate, and I happen to know that Cadbury Dairy Milk is your favourite chocolate 'in the whole world', I believe you said. You can never resist it! SO! That means that you are definitely in shock! SO!

Tell you what; you eat the chocolate and… I… *won't* tell mum that you had some freak out, and almost died…leaving Lily ALONE in the house".

Nathan tries - and fails, to suppress a laugh. Jake looks at me, his face still annoying calm, but with a bit of humour emerging in it.

I sigh dramatically, and open the chocolate bar. At that point all four of us look at each other and burst out laughing. And maybe our laughter is strained, but it is something we do anyway. To lighten the mood.

But to my own ears, my laugh sounds hollow.

My mind and eyes turn to Nathan.

With surprise and a little bit of shock, I realise that his laugh mirrors and reflects my own.

(10) Nathan

So, this was an interesting day for me.

I was just planning to go round Jake's house, do some A-level revision, you know, a normal, nothing- out - of - the - ordinary day.

But I end up saving a relatively hysterical girl from being run over, and she turns out to be Jake's younger sister. Wow. Great. *Awkward* - for her and me.

Seren sits across from me now, gazing into the cup she holds tightly, as it's her lifeline to reality.

And sanity I dryly add. But I know that's not fair. It's just when I grabbed hold of her, she had an expression in her eyes that I had never seen in anyone. It was kind of far away, as if she was re-living something from her past. But it was also scared, as if she didn't want to re-live whatever she was re-living. They were ... slightly blank, as well, as if she didn't really *care* about reality. Within them, I could see flickers of unspeakable grief.

And then she blinked, and the far away and scared expressions were gone. And for me the scariest part was that her young eyes, they mirrored mine.

Seren looks up at me, and smiles awkwardly. She clears her throat. "Um, I owe you a thank you and a... explanation".

I jump in.

"You don't need to explain anything".

She shakes her head "I think I do... Listen, I'm not usually like *that."*

She stops to take a breath. "Someone, I was pretty close too... isn't ...um... in my life anymore... and..." She looks up.

"I'm having a pretty rough time dealing with it...and..."

Before Seren says anymore, I interrupt her *again*.

"Look, don't say anymore, you don't need to...I understand".

Seren looks grateful and tries an awkward smile - which I am probably mirroring.

"How about we just forget about it?" I suggest.

Her smile loses the awkwardness, and she nods.

"I'll like that".

(11) Seren

So, after (politely) chucking Nathan out of the house, when they finished their revision, Jake turns his attention to the frozen wasteland we call a freezer, looking for something we can define as edible.

"Seren!" he yells out.

"What?"

"You okay with Sweet and Sour Chicken? -It's your favourite isn't it?"

Wow, I'm surprised. Jake found something good in that freezer.

"You know it's my favourite, Jake".

I hear Jake drop something, then curse. He yells again.

"Well, tough, we don't have any".

After finding three microwavable meals of Chicken Tikka Masala (Jake's favourite), Jake flops down next to me on the sofa, turns on an episode of Doctor Who and groans with annoyance.

I turn to him "If you're groaning because you think Matt Smith is an awful Doctor, then you can keep your mouth shut".

He raises his eyebrow "Wow. Aggressive".

He then rolls his eyes.

"No, actually, I'm groaning because my mind is too shattered to cope with the time travel complications of Doctor Who, after Nathan trying to explain Calculus to me".

I frown. "What's Calculus?"

He shrugs. "No clue".

I roll my eyes this time.

"That's helpful" I snort, and turn my attention to Doctor Who. Matt Smith is currently trying to reason with a Dalek.

Jake stays silent for a few seconds. But I can, out of the corner of my eye, see him start to fidget.

The storm is about to begin....

So I start talking-quickly. "Nathan seems...nice then. He's....what, eighteen? I'm guessing he's clever if he can help YOU with Calculus".

Jake stays silent. He would usually laugh.

"You met him at St Johns, right?"

"Seren..." Jake begins slowly.

"Do you think Peter Capaldi is a better Doctor than Matt Smith? What about David Tennant? He was good. God, I remember a friend and me found it really funny that a Scottish man was going to be the next doctor, and then there was the Scottish referendum! Isn't David Cameron trying to organise-"

"Seren" Jake says, interrupting. "Please shut up".

I sigh. "Can we not bring up today?"

Jake looks at me with pity and sympathy.

For some reason, this makes me feel slightly angry. It's almost as if he's trying to patronise me.

"Seren, I think we have too".

I shake my head-firmly and forcefully. "No. No, we really don't".

I refuse to look at him. I hear him sigh. He seems to be doing that a lot lately.

"Alright, Seren, fine - *fine.* Problem is, we're - I'm getting worried!"

I turn to him, pretending to be confused. "About what?"

He stares at me in frustration (and disbelief). "Today was the first time, you went outside in 21 days!"

I shrug "We live in Britain - it's rainy and cold".

"You're pretending to be stupid, and we both know it! Britain being rainy isn't the point!"

I glare at him. "Then what is? Because if you've got something to say, just say it!"

I don't usually get angry with Jake, but I'm having enough. I don't want to think about it, talk about it, or even mention it. I thought that was clear.

Jake doesn't back off. He stares at me for a few seconds, and then his jaw hardens "You know what? Fine! I'll say it: You're not moving on! You're living in the past, you can't even hear the name 'Daniel' without flinching! You're making yourself sick!"

Just like Jake said, my body automatically recoiled when he said that name. Almost like that his body falling back...when it...

"Shut UP, Jake!"

But he carries on. "For God's sake, you can't live like this! Don't you get it?! Nothing's going to get better unless you try! You need to talk to your friends, or you're just gonna push them away, and you're going to get bloody worse! And Ally needs you! She might relapse any moment! And *you* need her, for Christ sake"- Jake pauses to take a breath "Please, Seren. Just talk to her!"

"I don't want to talk to her!"

Jake sighs exasperated. "Why bloody not!?"

"BECAUSE IT'S HER FAULT!" I suddenly scream "I didn't want anyone to die, but somebody had too!" I realize I'm crying now, and I'm angry, but the feelings I've kept hidden and didn't admit to myself are being released.

"Somebody had to die! And Ally knew it was her! She was ready- even though I wasn't! She called me, she wanted to see us, say goodbye, and I refused to believe she would actually go - she couldn't!! But we were walking to the hospital, and I walked ahead - into… the …road and there was a car coming…." I break off, breathless, try to breathe.

"It should have been me. I should have died, so that Ally could…live. But Daniel… he grabbed my hand, pulled me back….but it…." I still can't say the words.

Jake's looking at me, an unreadable expression on his face. "Oh, God…Seren…"

But I can't stop. Along with my tears, it pours out.

"Ally lived, but he didn't!! She got better, because he…died! For her! For me! And I know that means it's also my fault - it's my fault, and of course it is! But if Ally hadn't called then, the car wouldn't have been there, and if she hadn't got sick, then nobody would have had to die! But if she had… died- which I didn't want either! …then Daniel would have lived." I stop, breathe again, and then glare at Jake "Now you know, now you know, the whole and utter truth, and along with it, what a total bitch and what I a total murderer I really am".

I don't remember getting to my room, but somehow I find myself slumped down on the floor, and my head pressed against my wooden bed frame. It hurts, but I don't move my head. I breathe slowly. It's dark, late.

I hear thunder, and rain pelting down against my window, but it also sounds like something tapping against it. And just then, a flash of lightning illuminates my room. Like my imagination has released images, best never seen again, I see a vision of the worst day. But I don't flinch away. I don't know why. The lightning recedes, but comes back again. This time, I see today, me standing in the road in slow motion, before I was pulled back to cold reality. I hear a familiar voice, and this time I know it wasn't my imagination. This time, I see something, someone that's not possible.

It's not possible, but this time it is. As if… I'm in a different form or reality, a few minutes slower, I stand up, feeling a gentle presence that I know I can't deny, but I can't believe. I cross over to the window, where the storm continues, but not like a storm I have ever seen before. My imagination isn't *this* vivid, but reality isn't this surreal. I place my hand against the cold glass, not quite believing, but still hoping.

And I believe, I know, I don't understand, but it's reality. The glass warms underneath me, and I feel another imprint, but I don't dare to look down, I keep looking forward, scared that if I look down, break the spell, the real illusion that is being formed will fade away. How can this be real? But it is. And I'm not alone.

(12) Daniel

I don't know. I don't know if this is real, or if I'm real. I don't know how it happened, whether I did it or someone else controlled how I fell back to the world. My world, but I think it was me.

I never believed in ghosts, but somehow I think I am one. I'm a spirit...am I? I don't even remember anything - just white, just hoping. And then... like a thick clear mesh, showing but keeping me from the world. I saw a car, and Seren. And I screamed her name, but she couldn't hear me, and she couldn't see me.

And now I'm here. Just outside her window - It suddenly feels that am I in some sort of Shakespeare play- Romeo and Juliet maybe?

Though technically that was her balcony...and they sang to each other-which I hope to God is not gonna happen here. I mean, not that Seren has a bad voice... it's just...

Oh Christ! Can someone please explain what the hell I am talking about? Just the presence of Seren, makes me go all crazy and stupid.

What am I going on about? What's the world going on about? Can someone explain?

Because, the rules about living and dying seem to be broken for two people on this planet. And why these two? Out of all the people on this planet, Why us? Why us?

I blink twice, and keep looking forward scared to lose her face for one moment. It doesn't matter that I can feel the heat of her hand against the glass pressing into mine. It doesn't matter. What does matter is the sweet, beautiful face that is all I ever want to see.

Is it real? Am I real? Am I still dead? Am I alive? Am I spirit? Am I ghost? How is this even rational?

But it all just drops away, because I really couldn't care at all, because all that matters to me, all that has to matter is the girl on the other side of the glass.

Who ever said the world, the planet, the Earth, ever was rational?

(13) Seren

Right.

I can handle this. This is definitely not normal, but hey, that's okay. It's all okay. How can it not be?

I breathe slowly. I'm not alone. I realise we've just been staring at each other for about 5 minutes, but haven't spoken.

"Daniel?"

He - the ghost - the spirit - the imagination-*Daniel* blinks slowly in disbelief - I think it is him, and smiles. I think he laughs but I can't hear anything.

I must have looked confused, because then he frowns, and begins to open his mouth to speak... and I want to hear what... I have to hear...

"Seren?"

I blink, and I'm still curled up on the floor. And Lily stands near the door, her hand resting on it, ready to leave. She looks scared, of me... "Are...you... okay?"

"Um..."

Of course it was a dream, it really couldn't be anything else. But my vision goes to my window - with that little bit of hope, I can never lose. It may just be my imagination, my wishful thinking, but there standing out against the unforgiving, never forgetting black night, is a perfect silver handprint.

"Seren....?"

For the first time since the .... *Accident.* I smile up at my little sister.

"Yeah, Lily, I'm fine".

(14) Nathan.

I still miss her. It's been almost two years, but I still miss her. Which is why I'm sitting on the roof, just outside my bedroom window, in the middle of the night, just after a storm has ended.

There was supposed to be a meteor shower tonight, which she would have loved. She never actually got to see one.

It's kind of peaceful out here. I mean, I live near a main road, so I can still here the cars driving past, but it's like I'm excluded from all of it, like it all doesn't matter. If only.

I really should go back in, it's clearly not gonna happen. The one thing I want do for Clarissa, I can't do. So I really have no idea why I'm still hanging out here. Maybe I'm still hoping. Maybe I'm just stupid. But maybe we all are on some levels.

So, I turn around and slide back into my bedroom. I guess I should really get some sleep, but my mind is too hyperactive to stop functioning. It's not even picking up certain thoughts - it's just like a constant buzzing.

So, I literally dump myself on my sofa, and turn my T.V. on looking for mindless entertainment, to either, try and bore myself to sleep or help my mind focus onto something I can understand.

After deciding to watch some Top Gear rerun, I hear my phone vibrate. Of course, I've managed to jam the bloody thing between the sofa cushions, where it is slowly sinking into oblivion.

So I'm forced to jam my hand between the sofa to try and retrieve it, fishing though popcorn crumbs, chocolate wrappers and I - really - don't – want – to – know - so - I'll – pretend – I - didn't – feel - it, my hand closes round a small rectangular object, which I immediately pull back out.

I shake my hand out, shuddering, and take a look at the text, that Jake has just sent me.

Sorry bout time, but Im still not getting the Calculus-its keeping me up. Ive been attempting to do it since u went home. How do I do Q3?

This is extremely insulting to my teaching skills. I quickly send a text back:

What u not getting?

He replies in about 30 seconds.

EVERYTHING! Possible to go on skype?

I wasn't gonna get much sleep anyway, I decide. So even though Top Gear is starting to get interesting, I switch it off, load up my laptop, and send a call request.

Jake accepts it, and I get an image of him turning away from the screen, talking to one of his sisters.

"Look Lily, just because she was being nice to you doesn't mean she's lost her mind.......... No, Lily, she really hasn't gone insane! ...I don't know why! Well, is she okay now? What was she doing on the floor though?... Lily, you can't use that language!... I am in charge until Mum gets back... do not use that word either! ...Go to bed!

Jake turns to the screen, and groans. "God, sisters are more irritating than maths!"

I laugh "You want me to go then?"

"No!" Jakes laughs back.

Starting to frown slightly, I ask "What was that even about?"

He rolls his eyes.

"I don't really know.... A few hours ago, I had a...um...argument with Seren, and she went upstairs. Then I sent Lily to bed, but apparently she couldn't sleep, thought something weird was going on in Seren's room, so walked in."

Jake takes a breath.

"Basically, Seren's found it hard to get on with Lily since Daniel...um left, so Lily was scared that Seren would say something, or just ignore her. But, Lily found Seren, on the floor, looking kinda blank. Lily asked if she was okay, and Seren actually smiled at her....so Lily got all freaked out!"

Jake laughs, a little uneasy.

But I remain slightly confused.

"Okay…wait, who's Daniel?"

Jake looks a little stricken.

"Oh crap! I never told you!"

Now I'm even more confused, but I'm starting to realize. Earlier this morning, Seren's eyes matched mine, in emotion. I hoping Daniel did just 'leave' like Jake suggested, but those eyes matched mine, and for one reason.

"Oh, hell. He was her boyfriend, wasn't he?"

Jake blinks, surprised I worked it out. "Yeah…yeah, he was… was being the right word. He got hit by a car. They didn't think it was serious, cos he was talking and everything, but they went to hospital anyway… and his brain… starting swelling, and bleeding…. and it was too late….Seren saw him die. Thing is, he was more than her boyfriend, he was everything to her, it wasn't puppy love or anything…"

His words hit home, and hurt me in ways only, Clarissa did when, she too left.

"Jesus…"

He nods. "Yeah, I know. I only found out the whole story today. Seren lost it, and gave out more than she wanted. Her best friend

Ally has - well *had*, I guess, Cancer. The day Daniel died, they were heading to the hospital, and Ally said she was dying - they wanted to see her... It was Seren that was in front of the car, she told me today, that she was completely prepared to die, she thought it would save Ally - you know, Life for a life, and all that bull. Either way, Daniel, he pushed her out of the way and it hit him...instead of Seren....and she blames herself for Daniel's death".

Jake hesitates. "It definitely wasn't her fault... but you know when Clarissa died?"

I stiffen "Yeah, I do".

Jake looks uncomfortable "How did you move on?"

I relax - slightly. But then inwardly groan. Jake has not realised it, and I guess he doesn't really have a reason too. But he has currently asked the worst question that anyone can be asked.

But I understand why he needs an answer, and why I have to give him one. So I try to express it in a few words.

"I haven't really....I mean, I don't think about her about all the time.... But you know, I still miss her....."

Jake persists lightly "Could you talk to Seren? It might, I don't know....help her?"

I shake my head slowly "I'm sorry Jake... I really am, but I still can't talk about it...not yet anyway".

Daniel nods. "I know that....don't worry about it". I know he understands.

He gives a small smile "C'mon, let's get on with this maths" he says, pulling out his worksheet.

"So I'm confused..."

I still can't talk about her, even to my mates, let alone someone I don't even know.

But maybe I should try...maybe.

(15)

None of that was meant to happen. It shouldn't have happened - so why did it?

It was impossible - irrational. But somehow it happened.

I didn't mean to watch. But my sight crash landed two streets away from where it was trying to go. And then the controls broke. So even though I tried to break away-though admittedly I didn't try very hard, I couldn't.

My sight did eventually go to who I was looking for. He hasn't changed at all. It still seemed like yesterday, even though it's been a year and a month.

People like us - though I guess you can't really call us that, we can watch, we can send messages, but we can never make direct contact. It's an unwritten unofficial rule - actually it's more than that, you just can't.

But it seems you can.

(16) Seren.

I know what a dream feels like. I may have been tired, slightly confused, and possibly delirious, but I know it wasn't a dream. I also know what imagination feels like, and I'm relatively sure it wasn't any kind of imagination, combined with my wishful thinking.

No matter how hard I try, my attention keeps going back to the small mobile that I've tried to put out of sight. The text message icon is still clear on the screen - I was kind of hoping it would just fade away, and I could kid myself that I never got the message.

But it's not going to work, I begin to realize. I drum my fingers first slowly, then picking up speed. I really don't know why I still don't want to talk to her. Maybe because I still kind of blame her, even though I know it's really not her fault.

But the stupid thing still remains right there and ...I...should really pick it up but....

Oh for God's sake! I snatch up the phone, and am seriously considering hurling the thing out of the window - when it starts vibrating, and yelling out something weird that Ally probably changed my ringtone to for a bad joke which, granted, I would have found funny.

But it's not Ally calling. Without thinking, I hit the call button.

"Hello?"

And the voice that comes out is... like the first star emerging out in the night after a thunderstorm.

"Who is this?" I ask, because I'm so afraid that it was really a dream, that it was my wishful thinking, that whatever happened last night wasn't real.

Please....please.....please.

"....Daniel?" *Say I'm right....please.*

The voice on the other end laughs softly and nervously, like he can't believe it either, and he speaks, with a voice that is more air than anything else "...Seren".

And then I hear the click of a lost connection.

The small skinny girl sits on the bench at the end of the park, drumming her fingers, waiting for me. She still wears a hat. She looks up, when she hears my footsteps, and gives a small nervous smile. "Thought we should make it a public place" She calls out dryly, and waves her hand about vaguely "You know...witnesses".

I smile slowly. I have missed her. I walk over to the bench, and sit on the other end. Ally doesn't make a comment. We both breathe in deeply.

She's the first to speak "So.... Hi".

"Hi Ally".

Awkward silence.

Ally decides to act first.

She looks at me, with confusion and curiosity. "Why today? You've ignored me for, like, three weeks! Why is today any different?"

I sigh, fidget. "I don't know.....I really don't. It shouldn't be..."

Ally looks at me, expecting an answer.

"But I'm guessing that I got tired of fighting a losing battle".

She frowns, head on one side. "What was the losing battle?"

I look down. "Trying to forget about you".

She's silent. "Well then".

I agree "Yep."

"Right".

"Left".

She looks at me with a little bit of amusement. Then makes a small simple statement.

"You blame me".

I start, or at the least, pretend to. "Blame you for what...?"

She laughs sadly, and looks at me with a face full of sympathy, understanding, and also remorse.

"Let's not play games. Somebody had to die... and it should have been me. And Daniel became the replacement...at least, that's what you think".

I stare at her "How did you know that?"

She looks away "I didn't......And I just guessed correctly".

At that point, I went a little hysterical. I don't why. Maybe it's because I fell for the most obvious trick in the universe, maybe it was the disbelief that Ally *knew.* Maybe, it was the fact that she knew, but was still sitting there. Maybe it was all three.

"I'm a murderer".

"No, you're really not".

"It's my fault...Daniel died....and it's my fault".

"Seren, it most definitely was not your fault".

But those words seem unimportant - flat and empty.

Just run. Make the setting harder, and run faster.

I slam my legs on to the treadmill, and turn it up to the highest setting.

Keep going. Don't think. Just run.

I just want to forget everything.

Run, Just Run, Run, Forget, Run, Run, Don't think...

I don't want to think.

Run....Run.....Run.

But when you don't want to think about something, it's all you can think about.

I have to be insane. I'm insane. Daniel's gone - he's gone. There's no way he can be communicating with me. He's *dead,* for God's sake. Dead - not coming back.

I force my body to go harder, faster. I ignore the burning, the breathlessness. It doesn't matter. None of it matters.

Pain is just an illusion - but why do we feel it so powerfully?

Run. Run. Run. Run.

"Seren?"

I'm literally slumped over the treadmill, when I hear that voice – I'm still trying to run.

I lift my head up - still hopeful, because that voice sounded so.... And I see Nathan.

Nathan, looking awkward and sheepish, one foot over the threshold, probably wondering whether to walk in or not.

He lifts up one hand "Um....Hi".

I'm probably looking just as awkward. "Hi Nathan".

I then become aware of the fact that I'm bright red, most likely sweaty, and sounding like Darth Vader - but I have no idea why I'm actually caring about my appearance.

Nathan lowers his hand, and looks at my face curiously "You were going pretty fast there, you know".

I smile awkwardly, then frown, realising something. "How long were you standing there?"

He shrugs. "Bout a minute. I didn't want to say anything - I was worried, that I would make you jump, and fall off the thing..."

I don't really know what to say to that so I don't.

I look down instead. "Right".

Then there's an awkward silence. Nathan's the first to speak again, but quickly, as he if wants to get it out as quickly as possible.

"When Clarissa died, I wouldn't stop running" he bursts out "I used to leave the house early, every morning, and just...run... I didn't want to think about anything. I once starting running and didn't stop until I was on the ground, after falling over a twig. And all because I couldn't bring myself to think about it".

He smiles wryly, and looks hard, but gently at me. At that point, he doesn't look like a teenager. He looks like someone from a different generation. "Trying not to think, doesn't solve the problem, Seren - It just makes it worse for yourself in the long run...no pun intended".

He sighs and leaves the room, not once looking back.

(17) Nathan.

I'm not sure what actually made me say all that to Seren. It's not really any of my business. But I guess, that I can't in good conscience, let someone get over it the same way I did – badly.

"Just who do you think you are?!" says a pissed - off, hacked - off, and just about any kind of negative 'off', voice from behind me.

I turn around to find Seren, stomping up towards me. "Who in the name of hell do you think you are?!"

I blink "I'm sorry?"

She's pretty much yelling by now "What is wrong with you? Why the hell do you think it's *your* business, why on earth do you think it's acceptable, for you, someone I've met *twice,* to stand watching me, and then patronise me, on how to live my life! I don't care what happened to you-I don't care about it failing for you-it works for me. I'm moving on from Daniel this way! Who the hell is Clarissa anyway!?"

"My dead girlfriend" I say flatly.

Seren doesn't move for a few moments, her body frozen in time. "What?"

"Clarissa died almost two years ago. And she meant as much to me, as Daniel meant to you."

Seren looks down. Her face gradually moves from many different shades of red, until it eventually turns white.

She, Seren looks up, with an expression unreadable.

"I.... shouldn't have said that... and I'm so, so, so sorry..."

.I lift my hand up, to stop Seren.

"It's alright" I say. "You weren't to know".

Her eyes fill up with tears, that don't spill. "

"But how did you know about Daniel?"

I debate with myself, for a few moments, but then I decide it doesn't really matter

"Jake told me".

Seren rolls her eyes, and sighs "Of course he did".

"He's a little worried about you".

She manages a small smile "More than a little bit".

"You two are pretty close, right?"

Seren nods. "Hmm, I guess you could say that. Mum works a lot - seems being a lawyer takes up a lot of energy and time. So, before Lily was born, it was always just Jake and me..."

"He must be a good brother?"

Seren smiles, embarrassed "Of course he is...to Lily too".

Awkward silence. This seems to be happening a lot with us.

"Clarissa died off a reaction to drugs" I say quietly. "And it was my fault."

She looks up confused. I can see the question in her eyes, so I carry on. And it doesn't hurt as much as I thought it would.

"I was a druggie. I took a lot. I was high most of the time. But Clarissa never took anything...she was way too... anyway, I promised her I would *stop.* And I wanted too- I really did. But I couldn't..." I swallow, take a deep breath and carry on.

"I had just come home, in a bad mood. I thought I had failed a maths test, I had worked so hard for... I had it all ready, when Rissa walked in, all smiles, and laughter. And it was the worst move ever....but I didn't want her to be disappointed. So, I told her it was paracetamol. I left the room to go to the bathroom, and when I got back, she was slumped on the floor, after taking some to try and get rid of a headache".

I look at Seren, who isn't looking at me in disgust.

"I did all the right things, called nine - nine - nine, CPR... but she died 23 minutes, and 38 seconds later...And later, they turned out to be paracetamol after all! I must have got it all mixed in my bag. She had taken too many...It was so stupid! It was still my fault. I threw all the drugs out, after that - they weren't important anymore-they were the reason the most important thing was gone. And I would never get high again, but... what did any of it matter? Rissa was gone! Not coming back! I didn't want to think about any of it. So, I went running, until I physically couldn't anymore. My Dad would have to come and get me.

The worst time, was when that maths test came back. I got an A plus. My family was smiling and all going 'well done'. But it just seemed, like the reason that caused Clarissa to die was so ...pointless. I took the drugs out, because I thought I had failed that test. I didn't know what to do. I bolted. I ran for what felt like hours. I ignored that burning feeling, I ignored the fact that I couldn't breathe. I felt like death, but I embraced it. I deserved it! Then I fell over. And I didn't get up. I just cried, and screamed. Falling over didn't hurt that much, but it showed how insignificant that pain, was to the pain of everything else. When I stopped, I looked up, at the night sky. And it was all clouded over. And it was raining. I was getting soaking wet, but I couldn't even comprehend it. Then, I saw a tiny star, shining through it all. One shining star".
"I could have seen an aeroplane, I guess. But I still don't think I did. I won't lie, and say it all got better after that - it didn't. I got home, and got sick. But it helped me realize what I needed to know".

I sigh. Seren looks up at me with wide eyes. At that moment, she reminds me of Clarissa. Not because she looks like her. Just because of those eyes. Clarissa's eyes were a deep green. Like entering a deep forest with sunlight shining though. Seren's eyes are a deep ocean blue on a calm day.

I continue. "So there you go then Seren. That's the truth - and that's why I said all that to you. Because I went there, and no one should make the mistakes I did".

Seren still doesn't say anything, but she nods slowly to herself. Somehow, I think my words have started to get though. She then looks at me.

"It doesn't mean it was your fault."

I raise my eyebrows "Yes it does".

"No" she shakes her head, and speaks firmly and forcefully. She could capture the world with that voice.

"She choose to take the drugs-she may not have known the risks she was making but she took them. It's wasn't your fault, because you didn't want this to happen. 'Fault' implies that you did it on purpose, which you didn't. In fact, in a way, it was no one's fault. It just happened. One of those bloody horrible, awful things".

I nod, and look at Seren, in her deep ocean eyes "Then it wasn't your fault that Daniel died".

I smile at her, (hoping she understands) and go back upstairs, towards Jake's room. To my surprise, he's leaning against the door frame, with his arms folded.

I stand still. "Did you hear all that?"

He stiffly nods "You never told me any of *that*".

I can't think of anything to say.

Jake surveys me, then nods, looking like his sister.

He walks back into his room. "Let's get this Maths done then - I'm stuck on question four".

(18) Seren.

"Lily, c'mon, let's go home! I'm freezing!"

Lily yells back from the swings "One minute!"

"No, NOW!" I holler back.

"50 seconds!" she screams.

I pretend to think about this. "20 seconds!"

She pauses, thinks, and then yells "35 seconds..... PLEASE?!"

I pretend to sigh and sulk. "FINE!"

Ally, sitting on the bench next to me laughs.

"You're a mean sister".

I turn to look at her. "How am I being mean? I'm giving her more than half a minute!"

We both laugh.

"So...how are you really Seren? Even though taking Lily to the park is really, *really* fun, there's another reason you asked me to meet you here, right? " Ally says quietly.

"I'm...okay, I guess.....What about you? You're the one that just got over leukaemia..."

Ally rolls her eyes. "I'm *fine.* Stop avoiding the questions".

I wonder whether to tell her, in case I really am dreaming, and it's just me being delusional. I asked her to meet me here, so I could tell her, because I felt like I should and I want too, but I still feel, that if I told someone, then it would stop.

I take a deep breath "I don't think Daniel *left*".

Ally looks at me surprised by the way the conservation is going, and raises her eyebrows.

She says calmly. "What the hell do you mean?"

"This is never going to work" I say for the millionth and one time as Ally carefully draws on the art pad, we 'borrowed' from Lily's room.

"Well it's not, if you're going to remain negative about it." She looks at me, grinning. "Besides, if you don't think it would work, why did you get the candles anyway?"

"So, if doesn't work, I can prove to you that you are absolutely mental".

She turns back to the art pad. "Blame it on the Chemo...okay...done".

She places the pad on the floor, and we place the candles around my bedroom. I carefully light them.

We then sit around the makeshift Ouija board that Ally decided to draw, as she figured that attempting to summon sprits in my bedroom is a brilliant, fantastic idea.

The door to my bedroom is shut, and my window covered up. The only light comes from the candles which flicker softly, and cast strange shadows over our faces.

"So, Ally, do you actually know how to do this?" I ask, slightly worried.

She nods. "Oh, God yeah, well I think so anyway. I mean, I've seen all those movies, and read the books, you know, that kind of stuff".

I stare at her. "You're basing this on films you've watched?!"

She shrugs. "What's the worst that could happen?"

I glare at her. "Oh, I don't know. We release Satan or get possessed or… something!"

She laughs. "Now, *you're* basing it on films! Besides, don't worry. I've also seen the Exorcist…. And my Dad has the local Vicar's number. Okay, place your finger on the glass".

I don't completely believe in possession and all that horror stuff, but if Daniel's spirit is really there, then what else is possible?

Ally puts her finger over mine, and begins to speak in a deep monotone, that sounds so serious, and definitely does not suit her. So, it makes me burst out laughing.

Ally glares at me (or pretends too), and waits, looking like our headmaster, for me to compose myself. Once I've reduced my laughs to spluttering giggles, she clears her throat and starts again.

"Whoever is out there, if there is anyone out there, we mean no harm, we just wish to communicate with the spirit of Daniel Luccan, if he is there".

Nothing happens. Ally fidgets. I look down at the floor.

Ally sighs, and prepares to repeat the speech again.

Then, the candles slowly go out one by one, leaving us in complete darkness, causing me to jump.

I can't see anything, but I can feel my finger shaking, against the cold glass.

It could have been my imagination, or Ally being stupid, but the glass jerks suddenly to the left.

Ally laughs with fear, and worry and also slight hysteria.

"Ally" I whisper. "If you are moving the glass, I swear..."

"Seren" she whispers back "I'm not touching it".

My eyes have adjusted enough to see that Ally is holding up both hands.

I swallow and breathe in deeply. "Okay then".

"Seren, do not take your finger off that glass" Ally whispers, and I hear her grab the torch that I keep on my desk.

I realize that we've been talking in whispers for no apparent reason, like we're scared the 'spirit' can overhear us.

She quickly shines it on the board, creating eerie-looking shadows that shine across my bedroom. "Okay, here goes: Are you the spirit of Daniel Luccan?"

The glass doesn't move.

Ally tries a different tack "When you were living, were you called Daniel?"

The glass still doesn't move.

"Can you actually hear me?"

This time, the glass jerks forward to the area that Ally wrote *YES.*

"Finally, we're getting somewhere" she mutters, she then tries again. "Are you Daniel?"

The glass doesn't move.

Ally frowns. "Does that mean yes, or no answer?"

"Ask another question" I say quietly.

"Do you think it's him?" Ally asks.

I stare at her "I don't know...I don't know." But what if it is?

Ally nods then turns her attention back to the board. But before, she can ask another question, I think of a question and jump in. "Is this completely my imagination...?"

But before anything can happen, we hear a loud

BANG

Ally swears.

And my finger slips off the glass.

And in the now - open doorway stands my brother, and Nathan.

Jake looks at us, with confusion, amusement and pure amazement, while Nathan stares at the Ouija board.

"What in the name of sanity, are you doing?" Jake asks with surprising calmness.

"Nothing" Ally and I say at the same time.

Nathan laughs. "What does it look like they are doing, Jake?"

Jake responds, giving me the strangest look. "I'm hoping my sister isn't that stupid".

Ally frowns, and says, slightly indignantly and also quickly. "And what about me? - I drew the board!"

A small smile flickers across my brother's face. "I already knew that you were that stupid, Ally. But hey, at least it wasn't a tree, this time!"

Ally laughs. "Yeah, I think the Chemotherapy went straight to my brain".

"You mean there actually *was* a brain, under all that hair?"

"I know a guy that works with a MRI if you want to check."

Jake finally does smile properly. "Can we check my very stupid sister, whilst we're at it?"

"Which one?" I mutter.

Jake looks at me with confusion, then his face darkens slightly.

"Seriously, what the hell were you thinking? Do you realise how stupid it was?"

Nathan continues to stare at the board, then finally looks at Jake.

"Why is it stupid Jake...?"

Jake looks at Nathan incredibly "You don't actually believe in that spirit crap, do you?"

Not waiting for an answer, Jake shakes his head and mutters "Let's finish his bloody revision before the house gets possessed by Lucifer".

Nathan looks at me with a smile, as he and Jake begin to walk away "I'm not sure what I believe..."

"The house wouldn't get possessed by Lucifer anyway...I probably would though..." Ally calls out as they leave my room.

Jake yells back from the other end of the corridor "And he'll drag you back to hell where you belong, Alexa!"

Ally thinks for a bit, then smiles. "I'll see you down there! Oh wait! I can't go back to hell - Satan has a restraining order against me".

As they all laugh, I look down. Instead of being on *YES, the* glass has moved to *NO.*

(19) Nathan.

Okay, so that was an interesting moment. Listening to two girls having a séance, and then watching Jake slam open the door, after Seren asked whether this was her imagination. God, who would ever have thought that would have happened. I didn't think about doing one when Clarissa died.

Once Jake shuts his door, stopping the insults between him and Ally, he slumps into a chair. He seems older than eighteen. "She's not ever going to get over him" he says flatly.

I shake my head. "Yes, she will".

He looks up at me. "She will, will she? She was doing a bloody séance, for God's sake! Seren never had any interest in any of that kind of that stuff!"

I look at him "She's…sixteen right? You're telling me she had no interest in the supernatural…ghosts and the paranormal and that sort of thing?"

Jake shrugs "No, not really. She would think about it, but she didn't really take much of it seriously".

"She never cared about it, I just want to clarify?"

He shakes his head. "She was completely rational!"

I ask another question. "She never believed in it?"

"No!"

"So, if her friend asked her to take part ..."

"She wouldn't have taken part, she would have watched instead".

I sigh, slightly impatiently. "Then, think about it! You say she was rational - I'm assuming she's also sensible - though I haven't seen any of *that!* You also say that she didn't believe in it- SO, if she was having a séance..."

Jake catches on. "Then...she's had reason to suddenly believe in the supernatural".

I carry on. "*And,* what's going to do that?"

He groans, throws his arm over his face. "She thinks she's seen the ghost of Daniel".

I nod. "She must have seen something pretty convincing".

Jake frowns, moves away from his arm.

"Buts she's imagining the whole thing! MEANING, she won't get over him! She's trying to talk to something that isn't even there!"

I shrug. "What makes you think it's not there?"

Jake doesn't move. "For Christ's sake, *you* believe in it!?"

I give a small smile. "I told you, I don't know...But I like to think I'm open minded".

(20)

Simple reasoning: If you don't look for something, you probably won't find it. That may sound really obvious, but look deep into it.

If you don't believe in something, you will never see it. Granted, those people who don't believe it, won't want to see it.

But unless you personally open your mind, you may never see anything that could open it more.

Anything around you, can be used to question your faith, belief or opinion, you just have to know how to argue it.

Anything around you can prove or contradict.

It depends on how you see it.

Maybe it's also the other way around, you can't find something, because you don't want to look for it.

And you really can't blame people for that. Would you want to look for something that would question everything you ever believed?

You need to be open minded to see the arguments. But a door half open, and a door completely open are both 'open'-just different levels of it.

Nathan's mind right now is half open. He recognises that there is something more to see, but his sense of rationality still blocks it.

Seren's mind was half open but now has unlocked.

Like Nathan's used to be.

But maybe, I'm wrong. Maybe no mind opens completely. And maybe it shouldn't. If anything can be used to question everything, then what will that mean?

One thing that is completely clear: No mind is the same. Every mind believes something in a different way, even if it appears exactly the same.

Every mind will interpret something, in many and slightly different ways.

But that doesn't mean that either way is wrong.

(21) Daniel.

I'm everywhere, and I'm nowhere. I'm nothing, but I'm still something. I just don't what.

All I know is that my name is Daniel Luccan, and Daniel Luccan loved a girl named Seren Ambern.

It's like looking through the world through a thin white sheet. I can see everything, but I can't feel anything, I can't experience. I can see and hear, nothing else.

But when you lose a sense, the others become stronger.

I can hear Lily laughing, a sound that's full of happiness, and reflects the innocence in her.

I can hear Ally's voice. Gentle. Full of curiosity. Fun - loving. Fragile.

Jake's voice. Rational. Calm. Caring. Studious.

....Seren's voice: Indescribable.

I don't even know what I'm doing anymore. I don't know what to do now.

So now I'm just some floating weird thing - do I still count as human? Like most things, I don't know.

When I actually was… you know, part of Earth, I didn't believe in any of this - supernatural, ghosts, spirits… and the irony is not lost on me.

But if I didn't believe in it, didn't believe in any of it, why did I come back?

'You don't actually believe in it, do you?"

Seren, with a laptop, balanced on her lap, and a Triple Science AQA Biology textbook, open in front of her, shrugs. "I don't know - I might do. I don't really think about it that much, to be honest. It's like aliens, they might be there, and they might not be. But who knows?"

I look at her, trying not to show my confusion. "But you're a science geek. Doesn't this stuff, like, call science crap?"

She looks up. "Not necessarily… I love science, because I think it's everything around us. Everything can be related to science - it's just how you look at it."

I don't say anything. It's hard to argue back with *that* logic."

Seren smiles, graciously accepting my defeat.

"NOW, is there any reason we're arguing about paranormal activity when we're meant to be revising?"

"Because I didn't want to revise, and you can debate for hours".

Seren rolls her eyes, and gets back to her work.

I wait for a few seconds.... "Seren?"

No response.

"Seren...?"

She carries on ignoring me.

I cough.

"Seren".

Nothing.

I nudge her textbook.

Still nothing, expect from a smile she tries to hide.

I pretend to sigh, and grab my own textbook.

I sit across from her, and we don't make another sound.

The silence we formed carries on, until the sharp buzz of a mobile phone breaks it.

I jump. "Bloody hell, is that the Game of Thrones theme tune?"

Seren instantly looks up panicked, because as Seren quickly jumps up, and reaches for the phone, I realise that, the ringtone that just went off, only belongs to one person.

Five minutes later, we walk down the high street. Seren hasn't said a word since Ally called, and her hand clutches mine tightly.

There's nothing neither of us can say, so we carry on walking.

"She can't go yet" says Seren, breaking the oppressive silence that has remained for the last ten minutes.

"Maybe she won't. Maybe… she's just being dramatic. Maybe…she just wants to see you, and she didn't know how to get you away from your revision."

Seren doesn't say a word and grasps my hand even tighter.

"You gotta admit Ally has good taste. Game of Thrones – this is why she and me get along. Remind me to borrow the books of her -Why are they marketed as 'A Song of Ice and Fire', but the show is 'Game of Thrones'? You know, I still don't see why you don't really like the show but you don't mind the books".

I know Seren wants to smile, but she whispers.

"But what if she is?"

I know what she asking, so I offer her what little comfort I can.

"But what if she isn't? Either way, we'll go to the hospital, and be there for every possible option that Ally takes".

Seren's phone beeps again, (this time, a line from one of Queen's songs - one of Ally's favourite bands). She quickly reads it, and her face changes instantly.

"Seren?"

She looks at me blankly.

"Seren?!"

She drops my hand, and begins to run to the hospital that is now in sight.

I guess what must have happened, and quickly run after her.

I'm just behind her when I see it. And there's no time to yell her name, or tell her to run that little bit faster.

Instantly, without even thinking, I launch myself into the road, and knock her away.

She falls onto the pavement, and looks at me in horror.

"But she's okay" I think "It's all okay".

And then the full impact hits me, sending me flying.

"...its fine...Seren...It's just a cut...just a few cuts".

But I know she's not believing it. And who would? I'm not even fooling myself, but I don't want her to worry. The words I just spoke, don't explain why I'm lying on the cold tarmac, unable to move.

"Hold on, it's almost here Daniel...Just hold on...Daniel!"

But, as much I want too, I just *can't.* I feel myself slip from conscious, and I somehow I know I will never wake up. I remember thinking 'Maybe Ally can live now'. With the last bit of effect I have, I say a few last words "Seren, I love you so much".

I can hear the ambulance finally arriving, I can still feel the tarmac underneath me.

And Seren's blue, deep, eyes, are the last thing my human self sees.

And her eyes were the first thing I saw this time.

(22) Seren.

I fling myself up, a scream rising in my throat, which I choke down. I blindly feel about, searching for my light. But I can't find it. My hand carries on searching, but without success.

I realise that I'm crying, but it seems of little consequence. I panic, knowing I'm scared, but I don't know of what. And I still can't find the light.

I'm disorientated and confused, and I can barely comprehend that:

I was only dreaming, and now I'm awake - back in the present.

I let out a sob, as Daniel pushes me away from the car that came barrelling towards us - me.

I can't stop myself from crying out as the full impact of the car hits Daniel and sends him flying.

Only he didn't fly. He hit the ground hard.

I'm not only dreaming it - I'm reliving it.

Daniel's hand is cold. He looks at me. He says something - but I can't hear what.

He tried to hold on. The ambulance arrived - he could have made it.

But his hand goes limp in mine, and his eyes shut.

Brown - his eyes were brown.

"Every time I see you, Seren, I think I will see dolphins and whales swimming in your eyes".

"Every time I see you Daniel, I expect to see a Cadbury logo in your eyes".

The paramedics ran. But they were only a few seconds late. Of course, none of us could accept that.

He was still breathing, his heart still going. Broken arms and legs - but he still had a chance.

What I didn't know, is that what made Daniel...Daniel, was slipping away slowly.

He died in the ambulance, when they were driving at break neck speed to get him to a hospital that could treat the injuries they suspected he had.

They did everything they could for him.

I'm hysterical now. My hands reach out and grab out at empty air. The darkness of my room seems suffocating.

I need to find that light. If I can find the light, I can force myself back into the present.

Daniel went limp. He was wearing jeans and a white top-that became splattered.

His Brown hair turned red.

His brown eyes that shined, went dull and glassy, just before they shut.

Everything's fast and everything's slow.

The light. Where is the light?

I'm scared, and I'm full of fear. And I finally know why. I'm scared of my own memories.

I choke down another scream.

My hands once again close on empty air. They fumble about uselessly, as if I can't control them.

I still can't understand where I am.

Suddenly, along with a thrust of air, my hands thrust in an opposite direction, and close on a small oblong object with a tiny switch.

A flash of bright, piecing light, shines and illuminates my room. The light stings and hurts, but it takes away the darkness.

I'm crying again, but more out of relief than anything.

I'm back in the present reality, away from the memories.

I gulp down more sobs, cup my hands over my mouth, and breathe deeply.

I gradually come back to myself, I gradually calm down.

Oh God. Oh God.

I need air.

I slide out of bed, and stumble over to the white windowpane, which I lean on heavily once moving the long blue curtains out of the way.

I reach out, and open it as far as will go.

I close my eyes and let the freezing, fresh air wash over me.

I'm okay. I'm okay.

I'm shivering. But I don't know if it actually is shivering, from the cold, or shaking from the dream.

Well, I guess it wasn't technically a dream. More like a memory. But God, I wish so much that it had just been my imagination.

I wake almost every morning just thinking that. And I still lunge for the phone when it rings, just in case...

But of course, it never is, and you feel so stupid, because you know it could never be. But you just can't stop yourself.

Oh Daniel...why did it have to be you?

I shut my eyes even tighter, as guilt begins to overwhelm me.

It wasn't Daniel that stepped in front of the car, it was me.

Stop. Stop. STOP.

I'm a murderer in all but name and law.

Nathan. He said it wasn't my fault. But how can it not be?

I was the one that stepped out. I was the one, who said we needed to get to the hospital that started running.

And Nathan has the nerve to blame himself for his girlfriend's death! How is it his fault?

He didn't force Clarissa to take the pills.

But I forced Daniel to save me, the minute I placed myself in danger. He had no other option - that was the only way there was.

Nathan did everything right - he knew what to do.

But I didn't - I was in shock, in panic. I couldn't even think.

Like now.

I open my eyes out of panic and shock.

On the window, vapour shows where I have been breathing.

I wait until I feel calm again. I then shut my large window, and turn away.

When it hits me.

The vapour. It wasn't showing where I was breathing.

Because it wasn't where I would have been breathing

It was on the other side of the window.

I walk back to the window, slowly. As I watch, the vapour expands, as if someone was breathing on it.

I step closer, and look out. Maybe it's too dark to see properly but its seems that no one is there.

Well, maybe no one *human* is there but...maybe...possibly....hopefully.

I shut my eyes, and just hope. Just hope it could be Daniel.

I'm almost scared to open my eyes again.

What if I do, and I find I'm still dreaming?

But deep inside me, I know I'm wide awake in the middle of reality, in an irrational situation, that has somehow happened, by some miracle.

I open my eyes slowly, and I can't believe what I see. For a moment, it seems as if a hopeful dream has blinded me. Like, when you lose something, and you try to find it. And you go to a place where you think it might be. And you trick yourself into thinking it's there, until you look again and you realise you were imagining it.

But I blink again and it doesn't fade away.

Someone has dragged their finger along the vapour. I suppose it just be the vapour turning back to water. But I have never seen letters forming when that happens. And it cannot possibly be a coincidence that it is five small letters, forming one word:

Seren.

Oh my God.

Just then my phone beeps once. Without taking my eyes off the message on my window, I pick it up. And read the small message that has appeared, under the other messages that my boyfriend has sent me, over the past years.

So. The supernatural is real then.

I realize I'm laughing, more than I have for 22 days.

The message in water vapour has gone. But my phone beeps again.

God, it's not that funny is it Seren?"

I frown. Feeling a little idiotic, I call out to the room "Can you hear me?"

I look down at the phone, and a new message appears.

No.

I roll my eyes.

Sorry. Couldn't resist........ YOLT.

"What's that meant to mean?" I say.

You only live twice.

"Oh. Very funny. I just forgot to laugh....How are you doing this anyway?"

I actually don't know. I just.....can. I haven't been able to keep it up for this long before though.

"Okay then....What's it like being a ...um.... Ghost? Spirit?"

Oh. It's cool. Weird. But it's cool. I can do things now.

"Um...Right.... Daniel..... I'm.....I wish I could....I wish I could tell you...or make you understand....the depth of my guilt and remorse. I'm so, so, so sorry. I love you...Ally lived. But you died... and that was my fault. And I can't make it right again...But you're here! It's not perfect...but it's okay. You're still here!"

I didn't force you to leave.

It takes a while for the next message to come though. He said he couldn't keep it up for long. I worry he's gone.

Seren...You have to read this very carefully. IT WAS NOT YOUR FAULT.

I read this slowly. And I know he's lying. It was completely my fault.

"You're lying Daniel".

SEREN. STOP DELUDING YOURSELF.

But I'm not. He is.

"Shut up Daniel! Shut up! Just shut up! It's my fault! It'll always be my fault! Stop trying to take it away! It's my fault - it's the only way it all makes sense! Why Ally lived, and why you died! There is always an explanation! And in this case - here it is! My fault!"

...**Seren... you can't explain everything that happens in the world.**

I'm not trying to, Daniel. Just what happened to you.

I'm angry, and I don't think about what I do next.

I yank off the phone backing, and pull out the battery.

Reason suddenly returns to me, and I think about what I just did.

"No... No...No"

I desperately shove in the battery and turn the phone back on.

"Please no. Please no...Daniel..."

I navigate to the text message icon, and from there, select the contact that says Daniel, and scroll down to the latest message.

But none of them are there. The conservation I just had isn't there. No record of it.

It's like I imagined it. It's like it never existed.

But I didn't. I couldn't have.

I think back to the séance, when I looked down, and saw that it had moved to 'No'.

It's not rational.

I could have knocked it. Ally could have knocked it.

But for some reason I don't think we did.

And for now, it's all I've got.

I haven't imagined any moment of this.

I could have. But I haven't.

I'm sure I haven't.

I hope I haven't.

I *know* I haven't.

(23) Nathan.

I stop walking for a minute. And just stay still. After this minute, I walk through the gate. I haven't been here for a while. But today it's exactly two years since she died. And it seemed right.

It's a relatively warm day, and the place is quite busy. But that's okay. We all respect one another, and why we came.

The cemetery seems more like a park, then a place of resting. And even though the road is nearby, the trees hide it form view, and the peaceful silence, drowns out any sound it makes.

I approach one of the small buildings that is situated slightly above the park. The doors are wide open, and I don't make a sound as I enter.

The room is silent, and full of different people, from different backgrounds. A mother with two children, a young woman. An old man that has to use two walking sticks and carry an oxygen tank.

I slowly walk over to the heavy, voluminous book that is displayed in the middle of the room. It is turned to today's date like I knew it would be. Below a picture of a Red Kite, is a picture of a meteor. And next to it, is Clarissa's name. I read the small inscription that follows her name.

Though my soul may set in darkness, it was rise again in light.

I have loved the stars too fondly to be fearful of the night.

'What my boy, you are not weeping, you should save your eyes for sight. You will need them mine observer for yet enough night' I think, remembering the poem. The old astronomer, Sarah Williams. Clarissa's favourite.

I stare at the book for a while, and then smile, remembering the time Rissa showed it to me.

I look out at the opposite end of the room, where the doors are wide-open, showing the park.

I take one last look at the book, and begin to walk out, onto the last resting place of the girl I loved.

I leave none but you, my pupil, onto my plans are known.

Past the trees, away from the gravel path.

Until I come across a group of four trees that form a clearing.

You have none but me, you murmur, and I leave you quite alone.

We spread Clarissa's ashes where she could see the stars she loved so much.

I walk slowly, remembering that Rissa never actually saw a meteor shower, no matter how much she wanted to. Every time, it was always never to be seen. I hope she can see them now.

Hesitantly, I enter the clearing. It seems almost sacrilegious. But I feel close to her here. I place down the bundle of white roses I brought. She hated white lilies, but she loved roses, even though she wasn't a total romantic.

"Why did you never come in spirit?" I whisper around me. "If Seren saw Daniel, why did I never see you?"

"Do you blame me for your death Clarissa?" I've had of counselling since her death and I've kind of accepted that it was one of those God - awful things that happen. But some days, I still feel that guilt. It's been two years, and I know it's going to take a long time, for the guilt to subside, but in some ways I don't really want it to.

I don't know how long I stayed there, but it didn't matter. It felt right.

"God, I miss you Rissa".

I close my eyes, and I can almost hear her name on the wind.

I straighten the roses I brought, and force myself onto my feet.

The moment has past.

I leave the cemetery a lot slower than when I entered.

As I walk over to where I left my bike, I see a small figure huddling into herself, as if she is trying to make herself as small as possible.

I change direction and walk over to her. Seren looks up, and gives a small hesitant smile when she recognises me.

"Hello" I say.

"Hi" she replies.

"You okay....?"

She nods quickly. "Fine...Are you?"

"Me... oh yeah, I'm good".

Seren focuses her eyes away "So...were you here for Clarissa?"

I nod "Yeah...it's two years today".

Seren looks down "Oh...I'm sorry".

I slowly shrug it away "Don't be... did you come...um...for Daniel".

She looks back up, and slowly nods. "I don't know the way around. I haven't been before".

"I can show you if you want".

Seren looks unsure "Oh, you don't have too... I'll just..."

I interrupt her "It's no big deal... its hard coming on your first time...C'mon".

I walk back into the cemetery, and Seren follows me.

But as we reach the doors to the small building, I hear an inaudible sound. When I turn round, Seren's gone.

(24) Seren.

I know it was stupid running off like that, but I just couldn't face it. Not yet. Seeing where his ashes were spread, would make it seem like he really did leave. And he hasn't yet. Not really. I don't think so anyway - expect he hasn't come for two nights.

I thought if I came, and saw his resting place, that I would be able to face the world again, without having to think about him. That maybe he could actually *rest* and we could both move on.

I open the door, and step into the hallway. I quickly make a bolt for the stairs, but Jake overhears me - which is what I wanted to avoid. He's too preoccupied with revision - and lazy to get up, so he calls out "Seren? How was it?"

I don't answer at first.

"Seren!"

I groan - I don't like lying, but if I don't, he'll worry and he has other things to worry about.

"It was fine!"

I hear the scoff. "Oh reallllyyy?!"

"YES!" I yell, already beginning to get nervous.

"Cos' Nathan just texted me".

Oh crap.

"Jake...I tried...but...."

I hear him sigh. "I know you did... you got to the cemetery at least. Maybe next time, you'll actually make it inside".

I don't really know what to say next, so I carry on walking up the stairs...where I bump into my sister.

She looks up at me innocently "Did you buy me some sweets?"

Oh right. I said I would.

"Oh sorry Lily, I forget".

She pouts. "You promised!" she states. Blocking my way.

"Lily, not now!"

"But you should keep promises! - you tell me too!"

"Lils- I had other things on my mind!"

"BUT you broke a promise!"

I've had enough of this. "Just shut up!"

I push past her -but place my hand out so she won't fall down the stairs.

I then run to my bedroom, trying to ignore her, as she starts to cry and trying to ignore Jake starting to call out.

The noise only stops when I shut my door, bringing a harsh silence. It's soon broken, by the sound of sobs that I can't control.

After a while, when I have calmed down enough, I hear a knock on my door.

“Yeah?” I call.

Jake walks into my bedroom, holding out his phone “Nathan”, he mouths.

I frown

“So?” I mouth back.

“He wants to talk to you” mouths Jake.

“Why?” I say, still mouthing - though I think I know why.

“Take the bloody phone!” Jake says - not mouthing.

I sigh and take the mobile off him. I place it up to my ear.

“Hello?”

“Hi Seren—again”.

I give a small smile “Everything okay?”

He coughs “Well, that’s what I was going to ask you. You know, um, about what happened at the cemetery. I meant to catch up with you –but I didn’t know which way you had gone”.

I blink - why would he have wanted to catch up with me? I barely know him. “Yes, everything’s fine. It’s just...you know...”

I don’t need to carry on. Nathan interrupts me

"It's alright, I do know... I did the same thing when I went for the first time... it gets a bit overwhelming".

The way Nathan carries himself and acts -you would never imagine like he lost someone - unless you know where to look. He absorbs it into himself. He stands tall-like he can face the world. I, on the other hand, is likely the exact opposite.

Nathan carries on talking. "I mean, I just wanted to see, if you were okay. I didn't see where you went - Jake said you were relatively okay, but...he, well, hasn't been in this situation....so..." He laughs nervously.

I smile. "It's all fine, really.... Thanks for calling...Um...bye"

I hand the phone back to my brother, who has been trying not to listen, but it's pretty obvious that he is curious.

He nods a thanks at me and walks out of the bedroom, talking about some kind of calculus homework, that he *still* doesn't understand.

Before Ally was placed in intensive care, I would visit her at hospital. Daniel, respecting that I would want some 'Best friend time' (as he put it) would walk me over, but then 'retreat' (as he put it).

But then, when I was home, he would call, asking how it all was and how it all went. I mean, Mum and Jake would ask if it all went okay. But Daniel was the only person that ever called- without fail.

He even called when I couldn't see Ally for the first time -when she had been placed in intensive care. He did that every day, just to see how I was, and how Ally was.

She was expecting to die at this point. Her cancer was spreading to her organs - it wasn't looking good. I had spoken to her on the phone, but I hadn't seen my best friend for more than two weeks. At which point, Daniel decided to sneak me into intensive care. That was the last time I saw her and heard from her. Until a couple of days later, when Daniel and I were supposed to be revising, my phone went off...

I found out Ally was going to be fine, 10 minutes after we made it to the hospital.

I was in shock. I couldn't hear what they were saying to me. Because my mind and body was focussing on one word. They sat me down somewhere - I don't know where, and tried to talk to me.

"What's your name, Sweetheart?"

"What was...What is that boy's name? Can you tell me that?"

Once they coaxed the information from me, they didn't say anything. A young paramedic sat with me - she was shaking, I think and crying quietly. She held my hand.

My phone went off. I grabbed it instantly- I thought - I hoped... that it could be...

But then I recognised Ally's ringtone. One thing you can say about Game of thrones is that it is unique. I thought - I thought that she had gone too. I was shaking, but I accepted the call anyway.

"He-hello?"

"Seren? Seren!" said the voice of Ally's dad. "Hey, it's okay...She's okay! She's fine! The drugs kicked in - she was speaking and everything! She's sleeping now - she was tired. But she asked me to call you. Don't worry, Sweetheart, she's okay - She's not leaving us yet!"

I don't know what I felt then - probably nothing. My best friend would be fine, and I felt nothing. Just numb. My best friend was okay...but my boyfriend wasn't. They were both sleeping, but one wouldn't wake up.

What should I have thought? Everything I could have felt, had a sharp contrast. I couldn't be happy. How could I be? But how could I go into grief? My emotions couldn't be for both people I had loved. I had to go one way, but how could I? Everything positive for Ally or everything negative for Daniel?

So, instead I felt nothing. Until a Doctor came, and kneeled down in front of me - he didn't have to say a word. Until Jake and Mum arrived though the doors. Until, I saw Daniel's parents running.

Everything seemed so meaningless. Everything was bleak and grey. I couldn't find one part of me that was positive.

I didn't go to the funeral. Daniel's parents didn't want a ceremony - they had a small (tiny) private one. Strictly blood relative's only - not even friends. Even not my mum, who had been friends with Daniel's parents for years. I couldn't face it anyway, even if I had been invited. Going to his funeral would have made it all seem real. It would drag me down to reality hard. And there were parts of me, that were still hoping that it none of it was true. I knew it was true. I knew it was real, but I couldn't accept it.

(25)

Can we ever actually realise what our actions will do? Even the small ones can lead to other ones, which lead to bigger ones, which lead to the biggest ones. Does almost everything we do set off a chain of motion? Who can tell? Some things seem little and unimportant. But is that because we don't realise what they can do? For instance, a small action, like buying the last can of lemonade in the corner store, can lead to another action for another person, who can't but that can. But this leads to a bigger action. He turns to go in a sulk. Even bigger action. Sulking, he doesn't think about what he is doing which causes him to bump into someone. The biggest action: He sees her face. He falls in love. All because another person brought a can of lemonade.

But if all those small actions lead to the bigger ones, are they predetermined? Was that small action destined to happen? Because the question is, what caused that action?

Small action: Nathan laid out a couple of drugs. Slightly bigger action: A girl saw them. Bigger action: A girl took them. Even bigger action: I died. Even bigger action: Nathan began to move on, after grieving. The biggest action: He saw Seren.

I want to see Nathan again - I do. I can watch him, but it's not quite the same. I can't say I see him - until he sees me back. But he can't see me. I watched him get over me. And he still blames himself - he always will. But his guilt is subsiding slowly - I'm pleased, as it wasn't his fault. It brings us back to the actions-was I destined for this? The actions lead to it. The actions could also have led to Seren-and I can't - I won't mess it up for him or Seren.

Nathan's letting go of the guilt that holds him back. The pain he felt starts to recede, leaving only the memories. I'll always his first love, but I'm a strong memory. And memories aren't always reliable.

He needs to let go of me. I want him too. And if I came back. If he saw me, then he would remember me again.

Letting the bad memories is good. Keeping the good ones is the way. With the bad memories, goes the pain, and the heartbreak. The good ones keep the good things.

The good memories that he keeps will go as well. Maybe not now, but one day he will wake up, and realise that he can't remember my face, or my eye colour, or my favourite pastimes.

And it's okay. It's the way it is. But at the end, all memories come back. When we step though that doorway, into the unknown. We remember who we were, what we were. At least, I did.

Before that though, Nathan will have a life. He will become someone great -he already is. I don't know what his chosen path will be - I could guess, but he will live, he will move on, mentally, spiritually, and physically.

But I don't what will happen to me. Will I remain like this for eternity? I'm a spiritual form. I have no body, nothing. I'm lighter than anything. I can see and hear the Earth, but I'm not part of it. I'm literally nothing. Nothing that should be able to think, or even have a conscience.

But I do.

I'm everything, and I'm nothing.

And I want it to end. I want to feel content, peaceful.

And I can't feel that yet. There's always something that I wonder about, always something I have to see.

And I can't stop myself. But I won't be content until I stop.

But it's not just. It's Nathan. I have to see him happy, and content until I can be. And I won't interfere.

I won't ruin this for him. He's so close. Almost there.

I can almost go. I can almost be free. But not yet. It's doesn't feel like a burden. It's Nathan. It never will be. I will never go, until he's ready.

(26) Seren.

I am literally scared of falling asleep. I am literally terrified of what will happen when I fall asleep.

So now I'm just sitting in my room, looking up stupid things on a laptop, reading a book, watching weird re - runs of a television show I haven't seen for months.

Anything to stop me from being tired, anything to stop me from wanting to sleep.

I can't sleep. I will not sleep.

When Ally was seriously sick, like completely on death's door, I visited her once in hospital. We didn't have to sneak in like before, her parents said I should see her in case it was the last time. The hospital board wasn't a massive fan of the idea, but her Mum used some interesting and quite amusing language, as well as some very entertaining emotions, and I was allowed to see my 'best friend before she might die'.

Anyway, Ally was in a lot of pain, but somehow she was still conscious. She said in a voice that can't even be counted as a whisper, that she was scared of sleeping.

Of course, I thought she meant that she was scared that she would never wake up.

But, that's not at all what she was saying.

She gasped out “God, why he is late?!”

I asked her who was late.

She looked at me with a small trace of her old humour but a dry seriousness I was only just beginning to understand

“Death - I’ve been waiting for a while-getting impatient”.

She was actually scared of waking up.

Sleep was the only true actual relief she got from her mental, physical pain.

She wanted to die in her sleep, so that she would never have to feel the pain again.

So she could quietly, finally, peacefully go without any fuss, any bother.

She also said that Morphine gave the most amazing dreams.

She could just simply float away, slip away, dream away.

She wanted that to happen so badly, but she never knew if it actually would.

She was scared of waking up, because she would have to come out of her dreams, and face her reality.

Face the pain of her body, of another day.

If she stayed awake, she wouldn't have to have the dreams, she wouldn't be put in the situation where death could come.

Ally is a fighter. But she also doesn't deny the inevitable.

She would meet death full on, she would shake his hand.

She would stand proud, but sad, as her soul would fade.

But, of course, death never chose her. She accepted this somehow, and fought her way back.

Like she always does.

Ally loved the dreams she had, when she was drugged up on Morphine.

But I'm scared of the dreams I will have.

They are always Daniel.

But I am scared of waking up.

So I continue doing whatever I am doing, in the hope that I will stay awake.

And I'm not a total idiot. I know my body can't properly function without sleep, but I'm not exactly thinking that far ahead.

And maybe, just maybe, I don't exactly want my body to function properly.

But of course, it doesn't work.

Nothing I do really does.

I'm still drugged up on caffeine, glucose and pure nerves, when I begin to slip.

It feels gentle, like a brief feeling, but then it becomes determined.

I'm fighting a losing battle with my own body.

It doesn't even feel like sleep. It feels like fear and defeat. Like apprehension and suspense.

It paralyses. I never thought about that. That's all sleep is in the end. It leaves you powerless and forced to experience the own demons in your head.

Part of my brain is still yelling and still fighting, when I finally unwillingly give in.

I'm with Daniel.

Eating at an expensive restaurant.

Laughing.

Arguing.

Being happy.

Then Daniel disappears.

A boy, familiar and strange drags me out of the earth, into the space. Around us are falling stars.

But he holds me, he stops me from joining them.

He looks at me with a strange seriousness, and whispers something.

"You are a star, you are a meteor. But you are not a meteorite"

Then I'm falling, amongst the stars, and Daniel is falling with me, but he can't reach me. He holds out a hand he wants me to take.

No one can.

And Ally is there.

And as I fall, she soars up high.

And Nathan is back, trying to stop me from falling. He holds out a hand he wants me to take.

And then I'm not falling. I'm amongst the stars. I'm alone, but I know someone else is there.

The stars form the shadow of a girl. A girl I have never seen, and have never known. But I know who she is.

She is tall, slender, and is a mystery. Her hair was long and blonde, her eyes emerald.

We are all connected. Our actions lead to something bigger. Everything we do will lead to something else.

Then I'm awake. And yelling and screaming into my hands that close around my mouth.

I'm confused again. And all I can think of is the memories I have just dreamed which I attempting to scream out of my body.

And yell out. And cry out.

Which is when my bedroom door slams open, and Jake storms in, holding a baseball bat, looking murderous.

For a spilt second, he looks confused when he sees no one else in the room. Then recognition dawns on him.

He immediately drops the bat, prises my hands away, and forces me to look at him.

But I can't stop screaming.

So it's not exactly a shock when his hand slaps me across the face, forcing me out of my hysterical moment.

We stare at each other in silence for a few minutes.

I speak first. “Sorry”.

He looks calmer than he really should be.

“You are lucky I didn’t whack that bat across your face Seren” he says completely factually, with anger, annoyance and worry creeping in.

He shakes his head “What was it this time? Some dream?”

I nod, not looking at him. “Something like that”.

I hear his muffled expletives.

“You need help Seren. You seriously do”.

He walks out of my bedroom, slamming the door. The worst part is, is that I completely deserve all of this.

When I next look at the clock, it’s around eight.

So I get changed, and listen at the door. I can’t hear anyone.

So I creep down the stairs, and run to that familiar door.

I get into a rhythm, and I don’t care that it hurts.

I turn around at the wrong moment, and find that I accidently left it open. And my sister stands there, looking at me.

She doesn’t even say a word, she looks scared. And she runs away. I hear her run up the stairs, and into Nathan’s room.

And I really, really wish I could go after her. I really wish I could care again.

And I really wish that going after her won't make her scared. That she could look at me like I am her sister.

I slowly get of the treadmill, and stand in the doorway, and I begin to hope I can make a choice. But of course I can't.

I shut the door, and walk back to that treadmill.

(27) Jake.

She really needs help. I hate to admit it, but she does.

My sister is losing her mind, and I can't help her, though I want to.

I'm sitting in my room, trying to focus on some God-damm piece of revision, when someone knocks on her door.

And I know its Lily. Because Mum's at work. And after last night, Seren is not gonna come speaking to me anytime soon.

I silently groan. I just want to focus on this piece of revision, though I really hate doing it. And Lily will most likely want to talk for something for hours, and will want me to do something, that will take longer, as I will have to explain why what Lily wants to do is not a good idea, why it will hurt her....and so on.

"Yeah, what is it?"

Lily opens the door, and I know something's wrong, because she opens it quietly and slowly.

She looks at me, with worry. And when Lily is worried, something serious is happening.

"Lily, what is it?" I repeat.

"Um" she begins "Seren's doing it again..."

I brace myself. "Doing what again?"

I'm not surprised when Lily finishes what she was saying. But I am disappointed, and slightly annoyed.

But I need to act like it's no big deal. Because, Lily is picking up on the tension in the house, and she is starting to wonder why her big, cool, awesome sister is acting the way she is. If it's a big deal, Lily will wonder more, and get more worried. She will be lost, confused and try to help which will make Seren's situation worse. She cannot know what has happened.

But she is not stupid.

So I pretend to relax. I even smile at her. "Oh, don't worry. It's fine".

She frowns. "But...you said...I had to tell you..."

"I know what I said". I say, still smiling, still relaxed. "But just don't worry. Just forget about it".

She's not buying it. "But Jake..."

"Lily" I quickly say. "It's all fine. Why don't you go watch some TV?"

She likes watching TV but isn't allowed to watch it a lot. So the fact that I'm letting her is what turns her frown into a smile, and what makes her run off.

She even shuts the door.

She doesn't see me lose my relaxed position, and drop the smile. She doesn't hear my groan or my swearing.

Last night, when I heard Seren scream, I should have realised she was just dreaming. It's not the first time she's done it.

But then she screamed out again. And I heard the yells, and the cries. And I instantly panicked.

I grabbed the first object I could find. The baseball bat was a memento of my own childhood, but it would do the job.

Mum, being a lawyer, was working late, so it was just me, Lily and Seren in the house.

Mum often gives me the responsibility of looking after Lily, when she's not here. Since Daniel, she also asks me to keep an eye on Seren.

So I didn't hesitate. I ran down to Seren's room, with the bat positioned high.

And immediately kicked the door open, completely willing to smash someone's face in, for hurting my sister.

I brought it up high. And saw that no one was in the room, apart from my sister.

And I felt anger. Then I felt even angrier for actually feeling angry at her.

I dropped the bat, violently, and forced her hands away from her mouth.

I could hold both her hands in one of mine, and pin them down. But she fought against me, with no recognition.

She was not fully recognising me, or what I was doing.

I know what to do with shock, and all things similar. But this was something else. I had never dealt with that before.

I know brothers and sisters are meant to fight all the time, try to kill each other, injure each other.

But that was the first time I have ever hit my sister. I didn't want to do it. I didn't do it out of anger. I did it because I had to. But I was still angry when I did it.

Because I knew at that point, that nothing I could do would help her.

I can't bring my sister back from the brink.

I don't why, but Seren and I have always been reasonably close. Which everyone we know thinks is really weird. Which I guess it is.

But the thing is, it never was just us two. It was always us *four* - Seren, myself, Ally and Daniel.

Our Mum was good friends with Dan's mum, and Seren met Ally at a playgroup. So we used to be together all the time.

Then, we thought that 'us four' would turn into 'us three', when Ally got diagnosed.

Then I thought it would end up with just me, after Seren and Daniel got together.

What Seren doesn't seem to understand is that she is not the only one who is affected by Dan dying.

When we were little kids, I knew Dan, better than she did. She was closer to Ally, which is, I mean, fair enough, we were kids after all.

She won't deny that.

But why she is acting like she is the only person who ever knew him?

And that frustrates me so much. I can't even show my own grief for Daniel in front of her, because she'll get angry, as if I don't have a right to.

I can't even mention his name.

Sure, Dan and I grew apart when he and Seren got together, and I started my exams, but he was always my mate.

He even asked me, if it was okay if he went out with Seren.

He was a little surprised when I was so...accepting.

What he didn't realise, was my logic behind it.

If my little sister HAD to have a boyfriend, which of course she HAD to have, I was glad that it would be someone I:

a) Knew.

b) Respected.

c) Liked.

When Dan died, it didn't even seem real. We were all expecting to lose Ally.

Seren was the only one who wasn't accepting the facts. She was trying to be optimistic. But even that was wearing thin.

I was out doing something with Mum - I can't remember what. She was driving I think, so when her mobile rung she asked me to pick it up.

I did it completely relaxed, the only thing I was actually worried about was if I could get an A on a mock paper.

It was someone at the hospital. Asked if we were the 'parents of Seren Ambern'.

Said my sister was at the hospital, with shock.

Then my own mobile rang.

It was Daniel's mum. She had tried to ring my mum, but the line was obviously engaged.

So she tried mine.

I looked at mum.

And, she was lucky not to get pulled over.

We needed to get to that hospital, to get to Seren, to be with her, just in case. To get to Dan's parents, to be with them, just in case.

Mum had barely parked, when I jumped out of the car.

We were running to the doors, when we banged into Dan's parents.

I remember hearing Mum trying to reassure her friends. But, of course, it didn't work.

How could it?

We were all running.

We ran into the room, just in time to see a doctor kneel down next to my sister.

Dan's mum and dad - I didn't see where they want.

I don't even know where mum was.

But I looked at my sister, and saw a look I have never seen before on anyone.

The look said that everything that made my sister's life worth living was going and gone.

There was a strange ringing in my head. Nothing seemed right.

I sat down heavily next to Seren. She didn't respond.

It was only when I took a closer look that I saw the tears running down her face.

She looked at me, and choked out some words. "Ally's alive".

I looked at her, confused. I was being extremely slow "What?"

She shook her head slowly, still crying. "She's going to be okay".

Then she completely broke down. Only at that moment did I actually understand.

And that's when it hit me. Who had lived, and who had died.

I felt the first wave of shock. But it was nothing compared to how Seren must have been feeling.

Mum took Seren home. I stayed with Dan's parents, though that's not quite true.

While they were talking about certain things in a small, private office, a quiet nurse led me down a corridor.

She then held open, a brown, normal door. Average sized against a brown wall. Nothing fancy. There was nothing about that door that could have described what was beyond it.

She let me go in alone.

When I walked in, I noticed the cold. But it didn't feel particularly different to how I was already feeling.

A lot of people say that dead bodies say that they looked like 'they were just asleep'

But, when I saw that body…that seemed like a load of bloody crap.

He was covered with a white sheet, which left his face uncovered.

I walked closer.

There was no way he could have been asleep.

He didn't even look like an actual person, more like some kind of model.

His face had lost its colour.

And he was completely cold. How can someone be that cold?

But I guess he wasn't 'someone' any more.

I still had some hope, so feeling completely stupid, I called out his name.

"Dan?"

Of course there was no response.

But I shouted it anyway.

"DAN!"

The body, that was Daniel, but not Dan, didn't respond at all.

But I said it one more time anyway, but flatly.

"Dan".

I have no idea why I went to see his body. I thought maybe it would make the whole thing seem more real.

And yeah, I guess it did.

But didn't help me in anyway.

I stared at him for a few minutes, just waiting for something to happen.

But nothing did, expect I started to feel the huge sinking feeling of Loss. Anger. Depression. Tension. Sorrow, that all blends together to form the emotion 'Grief'.

Mum picked me up. And as soon as we got home, I walked up to my room, and stayed there.

I didn't want to speak to my family. People who had known him as well. I didn't have the right to show my grief in front of them, and I didn't want to.

Then I thought about Ally. Did she know? I doubted.

So, I called her mobile number, she picked up immediately, knowing something was wrong.

"Jake" she said instantly. "Seren's not answering my calls, neither is Daniel. ...And a nurse just passed by crying about a boy...dying... please...please....please...don't..."

I took a deep breath. "Ally".

And then Ally knew.

We stayed on the phone for a little longer, but the two of us didn't really want to talk. We didn't say anything, apart from a few 'you still there?"

The irony of that wasn't lost on me. I was saying that to a girl, that almost 'wasn't there' anymore, that had been dying.

Knowing Ally, it wasn't lost on her either.

Eventually she choked out. "He'll be in Heaven. Satan has a restraining order against him...he said as much to me once".

Some people would call Ally heartless for saying something like that, but it made me smile. Call *me* heartless, but I knew why she said it, and I responded likewise.

"Oh no, Ally. He's saving the restraining order for you".

I could hear her smile, though her tears on the other end of the line. "I've been to hell, you know Jake. It was boring, no-one to annoy. So I came back, to drive all of you completely insane".

"You mean we actually have some sanity?"

"There is no point in driving yourself mad trying to stop yourself going mad. You might just as well give in and save your sanity for later." she quoted.

"Where's that from then?" I said, though I thought I already knew.

I could almost see her smile. "Douglas Adams-Part of 'The Hitchhiker's Guide to the Galaxy' series-The actual book though is called: Life, the Universe and Everything".

"Your favourite books aren't they? I really need to read them."

"Yes, you really need to".

Then she hung up.

I met Nathan a few days after that. I mean, I had seen him around before-same school after all, and we went to the same St John's group. We had exchanged a few words before in a particularly heated debate class, but I didn't know him.

I joined an after school revision session. I told mum when to pick me up, and said that I was going to try and get an A* in Calculus. She shrugged 'okay then', because for obvious reasons she was more preoccupied with her almost - comatose daughter, and her completely - confused other daughter.

But the real reason is that I didn't want to go home, and have to face my harassed mother, my almost comatose sister, and my completely confused other sister.

I arrived slightly late, so the only seat still available was one next to Nathan. So I took it, and nodded hello to him.

He nodded back slowly.

We didn't say anything. Until I realised that I did not know how to solve the calculus problem, and I looked over, and saw that Nathan had completed the whole sheet.

He was also looking at my sheet. He noticed, that I had noticed, and quickly looked away.

Which made me burst out laughing. Which caused Nathan to burst out laughing. Which caused the revision session to stare/glare at us with expressions of annoyance, anger, confusion and amusement.

Once we had calmed down, Nathan showed me how to solve the problem. And then showed me how to solve the entire sheet.

And I don't know. Like Dan, I had always found it hard to be sociable. But, maybe I just wanted a friend. I didn't realise that Nathan was looking for the same thing.

I don't listen to rumours, but it's kind of hard not to hear them. So I knew a little bit about Clarissa. I knew there was something more, but I didn't ask. There was nothing to ask. And it doesn't matter how someone died, whether it was cancer, a car crash, whatever. What matters is the effect that death leaves on the people that were left behind.

(28) Seren

I just want to lie here, on my bed, in the quiet, and pretend nothing else is real or matters.

Maybe, I'll start to believe it, if I stay here long enough.

Maybe, I can start to imagine things, and it won't matter if they are real or not.

No one else is here. Mum's working. Lily's at some sleepover I think.

Jake's gone somewhere with Nathan. I don't know where. But if I close my eyes, I might be able to convince myself it doesn't matter.

But I worry.

The treadmill wasn't working today. My thoughts kept turning back to something else. I couldn't stop them. But I can't stop asking myself, was I really trying to, block them out?

Am I still trying to make myself feel numb, and worthless, and empty?

Or, am I focusing on something else entirely?

So, I'm trying this instead.

I want to hear the noise that emptiness makes.

The noise inside your own head, where there is nothing else to listen too.

I don't want the noise of life. The cars that go by. The call of birds. The chatter of people walking outside in the light.

It's almost working.

I barely notice the sound of the phone suddenly beginning.

I ignore it. It's annoying, but it will stop eventually. Everything always does.

And sure enough, it does.

But begins again.

This time, if possible, it sounds more urgent, more panicked, more rushed.

But it all doesn't matter. Nothing does.

I let myself draw into myself. Ignoring life.

It seems like a more blissful version of sleep.

And then I'm awake.

And the doorbell is frantically ringing outside.

And someone is calling panicked.

It takes a minute, but I realise he is calling my name.

I also realise I know that voice.

The third thought comes quickly: Then where the hell is Jake?

And I realise that somethings do matter.

I'm running to the door immediately, and I unlock it, and fling it open.

Nathan stands there.

His face is worried, panicked and scared.

But the scared look disappears when he sees me standing there.

He begins to talk.

"Seren...please, don't panic-"

But I interrupt him. When people say 'don't panic', it's never anything good.

"Nathan, where's Jake?"

His face now looks surprised.

"How did you...?"

That confirms it.

"Nathan, where the *hell* is *my brother?"*

Nathan instantly puts his hands up "Seren, everything's fine-he's fine!"

"What happened?"

Nathan drops his hands, and looks down "He got...bumped... by a car. Look, trust me, he's completely fine! Trust me, he got a mild concussion, so he's in the hospital. Your mum asked me to come and find you. Trust me, he's okay!"

I do trust him. I do. Jake's fine. I believe him.

But he carries on.

"Seriously, he was on the ground, didn't get up, and just said 'Don't worry, I'm fine. I'm fine'. Then he picked himself up".

And that's when I just want it to end.

When I wished I could pretend that nothing ever matters.

But at that moment, I know I could never do that.

I am under strict instructions from Jake (via Nathan) and my Mother (via her mobile) to NOT go to the hospital. Jake is absolutely fine and it would just panic me out, which as Jake said (via Nathan) is 'the last thing ANY of us need'.

So, now I am sitting in the living room. Nathan is opposite me, because he refuses to leave me alone, in a time like this.

I looked at oddly "You said he was fine...."

Nathan nods "And he is. He asked me to stay...and I..."

He breaks off before he finishes his sentence. But his face speaks volumes.

I would have stayed anyway.

Nathan did everything he could. He went with Jake to the hospital and then called our mother, using Jake's phone.

He did everything I should have done. Because it was everything Jake would have done for me.

Last time, Nathan was here, Lily was also here, chatting in her normal way, and reduced the tension in the room.

Now, without her here, the tension and awkwardness dramatically increases.

It seems that Nathan notices it too. Of course he does. We could cut knifes with the atmosphere in here.

Nathan looks around, and appears to be listening out for something...or someone.

"Lily's not here?" he asks curiously.

I shake my head "No, she's at a Disney Princess themed birthday sleepover- dress up and everything".

Nathan smiles. "She went as Elsa or Anna, didn't she?"

I don't realise I'm smiling until it's too late. "Actually no. She hates Frozen".

Nathan laughs right out. "You are telling me that your sister is the one child on this planet that hates Frozen?"

I laugh too. "Yep, I am. She can't stand Frozen. She thinks the songs are annoying, and it's just a copy of the Lion king".

Nathan considers this. "Well, I haven't seen it...so I can't make a judgement. But if it's not Frozen, then what IS Lily's favourite Disney film?"

I don't even have to think about this. "Favourite Disney PRINCESS film is Tangled. Favourite Disney animal film is definitely The Lion King, and favourite Disney film overall is The Jungle Book".

Nathan smiles at that. "I have never heard anyone Lily's age say that the Jungle book is their favourite Disney film".

"That's my sister for you. She always been amazingly different than others..."

Nathan looks at me with a look that no one has given me for at least three long weeks.

"I can imagine...she's a lot like her big sister" he says softly, but casually.

But it still makes me uncomfortable. Quickly, I change the subject.

"Um...now that we are on the incredible topic of Disney films...what's your favourite?"

Nathan blinks at me, then seems to get a strange obsession with his shoes.

"C'mon Nathan, what's your favourite Disney film?"

"Embarrassing".

I laugh. "Disney films are *never* embarrassing".

Nathan looks back at me, with a glint in his eye,

"Alright, Seren, I'll tell you mine if you tell me yours".

I pretend to consider this. "Deal".

"Okay then".

Nathan coughs and looks away. 'Pinocchio".

I stare at him. "How on earth is Pinocchio embarrassing?"

Nathan stares back at me.

"How is it not?...Anyway, you said you would tell me yours..."

I nod in agreement. "I did... hmm... my favourite Disney film is 101 Dalmatians".

Nathan nods in approval "A very good choice. 101 Dalmatians is a perfect classic".

"I think Pinocchio is a very good classic too".

Nathan pretends to glare at me.

"Why do you find it embarrassing?"

Nathan thinks "I don't really know why to be honest. It's just one *those* situations. You know, when you think someone else is going to say something so effectively intellectual and ...supreme, and you've just said something that is the cheesiest thing since American burgers and its so cliché as well. At that moment, you realise that it has racist and demeaning subplots".

I laugh "I didn't think you cared what people thought".

"Well" he shrugs "I don't usually...but you know, I have my moments..."

I smile "We all do".

And we both laugh.

And we stop laughing. So we smile, which soon becomes awkward, as once again we do not know what to say to each other.

(29) Nathan.

It's almost disturbing how often I seem to be having awkward silences with Seren. This is at least the third one in about a week.

But it does seem that we are getting better at maintaining some sort of conversation, at the very least.

I mentally study the living room we are both sitting in. It's a reasonably large room that seems to have connotations of family. It's painted a sort of beige colour, which instantly makes the room feel warm. But this may be due to the fireplace in the corner that has an electric fire, instead of a real one. The carpet is a light red colour which just seems to suggest comfort.

There are two sofas, arranged to form a right angle. An armchair sits between them. Seren is sitting, kind of stiffly, on one sofa, whilst I sit on the other, just as stiffly.

There's a 'family-sized' TV, against the wall. But also bookcases - almost everywhere.

The French windows, and the other white, large windows make the room feel open and bright.

It just seems friendly.

And there are so many photos of Jake, Seren and Lily all over the room. A tall woman, who looks like Jake and Seren stands with them. I'm guessing she's their mother.

There are also photos of four teenagers standing together. I recognise Ally and Jake instantly. Ally's wearing a hat. But it takes me a little longer to realise the happy- looking auburn haired girl, aged about fourteen (?) is actually Seren. She's looking at Ally, a little worried, but also holding the hand of who I assume is, Daniel. Even though she's worried, you can see the smile in her eyes.

I study Daniel. He's tall, about six foot, I would say. Quite muscular, with brown hair and eyes. He's wearing an Arsenal football shirt.

"Arsenal was his team". Seren murmurs suddenly.

I jump. I realise Seren has been watching me study the photo.

I must have looked slightly embarrassed, because Seren shakes her head and waves her hand, mouthing 'its fine'.

"He liked football, then?"

She nods, smiling wistfully "And Rugby, and Badminton and Tennis. But not wrestling. He thought it was just violent and pointless".

"I'm with him there".

She laughs softly "He once made a point of actually boycotting WWE matches. Turned off the TV every time a match was on, even if he was on completely different channels. Not that he actually watched a lot of TV".

"Was he any good at sports?"

Seren nods her head violently "Of course, he was. But he wasn't a… you know, a typical 'boy', if you know what I mean. He liked sports, like everyone else…but in other ways, he was different".

"How so?"

Seren lifts her shoulders up in a small shrug, and begins to…sort off…curl up into herself, trying to make herself smaller.

"Nathan, can we talk about something else?...Please?"

"Yeah, yeah, of course, of course!" I instantly say.

Seren gives a brief nod, and doesn't look at me, just keeps looking down.

I then notice something on the corner of the room, next to a bookcase. But this bookcase isn't full of books, it's full of records.

"My God, is that a record player?"

Seren jumps, startled, and follows my gaze. She finally smiles.

"Yep, it is. My parents absolutely love music...it was a present from my Dad to Mum, on her birthday. Jake and I picked out some of the records...much to his annoyance".

I smile. I haven't seen a record player for…two years.

Seren seems to notice my interest and curiosity. She uncurls and gets off the sofa. It may be my imagination, but she seemed slightly unsteady at first.

“What kind of music do you like?” she asks as she walks over to the player. “There’s a music shop, down in High Wycombe. They sell records of modern bands, like Mumford and Sons. Of course, we couldn’t resist buying ‘old’ records as well”.

She kneels down on the carpet, to look closely at the records, stacked on shelves underneath the player.

I think. “I’m really easy going when it comes to music. Just DO NOT play any electronic dance music or Rap”.

She turns and faces me, after fiddling with the player “Oh, don’t worry about that. I can’t stand that kind of music…if it can be counted as music”.

She smiles tentatively. I laugh softly.

Seren turns to the records, and picks out a record from the top shelf. She glances down at it, and slowly nods to herself.

She slots in, and with careful precision, she brings down the needle on to the record.

About a second later, the music comes out, surprisingly loud and clear.

I recognise the band as Queen, and laugh.

"You don't like Queen?" Seren asks, sounding nervous.

I laugh "No, no, I love it. I just...haven't heard it in so long".

Seren looks down. "I love it too."

I would smile if she would look.

At least, now we have an excuse for silence,

"Daniel loved it too" she says suddenly.

I stare at her, and she starts talking quickly, faster than what I thought was possible.

"And so does Jake. And Ally. Ally really loves it, although not as much as Mumford and Sons. They're her favourite band. There's a record of Mumford and Sons here actually-should I turn that on?"

"No, that's alright. Queen's good...unless of course you want too?"

She doesn't reply, or make any kind of indication that she heard. Instead, she yanks off the needle, cutting off Queen mid track. I notice she's slightly shaking.

She tries to put the record back in its plastic cover but it seems her hands are shaking too much.

I don't remember getting up, but with St John cadets, it's sometimes an instinct. I kneel down to next to her, taking the record and cover of her. My hands touch hers in the process. She doesn't respond at all, just looks at me, despairingly.

"It's alright, I'll do it" I say, as I slot the record back in. I place it back where I thought I saw Seren take the record.

Seren looks down as I turn back to her, almost like she is scared to meet my eyes.

What scares me the most is that she is not even crying or shaking anymore. She is just kneeling there, like she has gone completely blank.

There's a blanket slung over the back of the sofa. I can just reach out and grab it.

I recognise it as the one Jake gave her, when I first met her. I drape it over her with still no response.

Once then, I realise that she has begun to cry. That's a good sign, I think.

I lift up my hand, and slowly place it her on her shoulder. She trembles slightly, but that soon stops.

There's nothing I can say that could help her in this state. She probably wouldn't hear it anyway.

So, we just stay like that. I don't know for how long.

Seren has just stopped crying, when we hear the unmistakable sound of a key in the lock.

Instantly she gets up, throws the blanket back on the sofa, and wipes her eyes.

With 50% regained composure, she walks over to the door, just in time for it to open, revealing her brother, and mother.

She smiles, like the moment that just happened, never existed. She jokes casually with Jake, and asks her mum a question.

Her mum answers, and then notices me, just standing awkwardly in the doorway.

She smiles broadly. "Ah, you must be Nathan!" she says happily, offering out her hand to shake.

"Nice to meet you, Mrs Ambern." I say, shaking hands slowly.

She laughs. "Aren't you polite! But please, call me Lynn - everyone does. Haven't been 'Mrs' since Lily was born...speaking of which, where is Lily?" She asks, turning to Jake.

Jake sighs. "At the sleepover. Remember? You had to buy the Baloo costume".

She nods violently. "Oh yes, I remember now".

Jake rolls his eyes at me. I smile.

'Lynn' notices this, and smiles too.

"So Nathan, are you staying for dinner?" she asks. "It seems like I am unexpectedly off work tonight, so I can cook"

Before I answer, I quickly look at Jake. He nods, mouthing *"Don't worry, it'll be edible".*

Lynn pretends she doesn't see this, although the smile on her face suggests otherwise, and looks at me inquiringly.

I nod. "If it's not too much trouble?"

Lynn laughs "Of course not, darling. Everyone here likes Spaghetti Bolognese, right?"

All of us reply in the affirmative, so Lynn heads off to the kitchen to cook.

Seren heads up to her room, and Jake and I head to Jake's, after Lynn yells: "Make sure he doesn't fall asleep!"

"So, you're alright, then?" I ask, as soon as we are both sitting down. Jake on his desk chair, me on his small sofa.

He nods. "Yeah, mild concussion". He shrugs as if to say *'What can you do?'*

"The hospital was pretty crowded, so they let me go, with a warning not to sleep for more than an hour without being woken up."

"That's going to be a long night".

He picks up an alarm clock that was previously on his desk. "Yeah, it will be. Luckily, I can set three alarms on this clock, and set another load on my phone, so Mum doesn't have to do anything".

He fiddles with it for a little bit, then looks up from it. "Was Seren alright when you told her?"

I debate with myself for a little bit, about whether to tell him the truth or not.

"Um, she was alright...but I wouldn't say she was okay".

"Ah, right!" Jake says. "She looked like she had been crying when I saw her...Did something happen?"

"She put on a Queen record. She said Daniel liked it, and then..."

Jake stares at me in disbelief. "But why did she put a Queen record on? That was one of Daniel's favourite bands".

"She didn't exactly say why she put it on, Jake. But it had been going on for literally about thirty seconds, when she started...panicking".

Jake puts down the alarm clock, sighs and gets up. "Thank you."

I frown. "For what?"

Jake gives me a look, and I understand now.

"Oh....you're welcome".

Jake nods, smiles and then begins to walk around his room.

"If she actually played the record, then that does mean she's getting...I don't know...better?"

(30) Seren.

I sit opposite my brother at the dining room table. Nathan sits at one end, whilst Mum sits at the other end. So, I've ended up siting between Mum and Nathan.

Mum's made an effort. She laid the table with the fancy, posh tablemats, cutlery and serviettes we only use when she's got her Lawyer friends over.

Jake and I do try to do dinner properly when Mum's working. But if Lily's not here, we just eat off plates in the sitting room (Not that mum knows that).

Mum makes polite conservation with Nathan, just getting to know him. Jake chips in sometimes. But I haven't spoken for a while.

Jake keeps looking at me strangely. He's noticed that I've kept silent for most of dinner.

Mum's noticed as well.

"Geography A-level seemed quite boring, when I was at school. But I bet it's really interesting now?"

Nathan nods. "Hmm, I think it's interesting, but I think most people in our Sixth form would disagree."

Mum laughs. "I bet they would! So, you and Jake are both taking Calculus and Geography? Jake's taking Maths, and English for his third A-level and his…AS- level-is that what you call it? ... Are you taking those two as well?"

Nathan shakes his head. "I'm taking English for my AS-Level, but I'm taking Biology for my third A-level".

Mum looks intrigued. "Biology…well, you're taking quite a diverse load there! *Seren*, aren't you planning on taking Biology for A-level?"

I jump, startled, and slightly annoyed. The whole table is now staring at me.

"I want to get through my GCSEs first, Mum".

"Which you *should* be revising for," murmurs Mum. "Although with your brains…"

I pretend to smile, not knowing who I am trying to fool.

"Um… what are you taking for GCSE, Seren?" asks Nathan.

Great! I have to continue talking.

"Triple Science, Maths, Additional Maths, English Literature/Language, Phil and Ethics, History, Geography, Spanish". I rattle off as quickly as possible.

Nathan blinks, and slowly turns his attention back to his food.

Jake stares at me, with expressions I can't place.

Mum inhales sharply, and talks as quickly as me.

"Did anyone get the post in today? No? ... Seren, go get the post, please".

"I'm still eating, mum".

"NOW, please".

Without making another sound, I get down of the chair.

I walk out of the dining room, into the hall and finally out of the house.

I have to walk down the drive to get to the post box, and I deliberately make sure the walk takes as long as possible.

I don't want to have go back into that room, where it seems that nothing has changed.

But of course, everything has.

I shuffle down to the black mailbox that juts out, almost into the road.

I shiver. I don't want to feel the cold. I don't want to feel cold. Cold is just a symptom of living.

Because if you never felt cold...you would never know what if would feel like to warm.

Warm when he wraps his arm, casually around you.

Cold, when he's not there.

But it doesn't make sense. How can he not be here?

I risk a glance up at the sky. Not one star. I don't know if that makes me feel better or worse.

"You can't keep acting like this"

I turn around, to find Jake walking towards me.

"What are you doing?" I ask.

He shrugs "Finished dinner. Realized you'd been got here for a while, so thought I'd come check on you".

"Oh". I turn back round.

"Seren, you can't keep doing this", he repeats. But this time with emphasis.

"We seem to be having conversations like this a lot, Jake" I say, trying to laugh, but instead it comes out strangled and hysterical.

Jake rolls his eyes, but remains serious "Because maybe we need too".

"We need to do a lot of things".

I hear Jake sigh.

"And there's quite a few things you need to do, little sister".

When I turn around again, he's gone.

(31) Nathan.

“So, both your parents are Math teachers?” asks Lynn.

I nod “Well, my Dad specialises in Algebra and Calculus, but technically yeah, they are both Math teachers. They also work in the same school.”

Lynn smiles “That’s interesting”.

Jake walks back in at that moment, smiles and retakes his seat.

Lynn looks at him. Jake looks back. Something seems to pass between them.

A few minutes later, Seren walks in, clutching a whole load of letters. Most of them have some official-looking logo on them.

Lynn’s face seems to deflate the minute she sees them, but then smiles a few seconds later. I wonder if Seren learnt *tha*t trick from her.

Lynn holds her hand out for the letters. Seren hands them to her mother, without looking at her.

She then sits back into her seat, staring at the remains of her dinner that has now gone cold.

“May I be excused?”

Lynn, distracted by the letters looks up for a second.

“Finish your dinner first”.

Seren sighs, “I’m not hungry”.

Lynn looks at her daughter “Fine then, yes, you can go. But clean the table first, please”.

“I’ll do it,” says Jake quietly.

Lynn nods “Thank you, Jake”.

Seren, without missing a beat, bolts from her chair.

We can hear her running up the stairs.

All three of us look at each other, and then look at the table.

Finally, Lynn sighs.

“I’m going to read these in my office,” she says giving a tired smile. “There’s ice cream in the freezer if you want dessert”.

She gets up, and heads towards the stairs.

Jake and I are left alone at the table.

Jake slowly gets up, and begins to collect up the plates.

I jump up and begin to help him. Jake nods his thanks.

In about five minutes, we’ve cleared up the table, and scraped Seren’s mostly untouched plate into the bin.

Jake leans against the sink, and sighs.

“What are we gonna do? She can’t keep this up”.

"I know she can't, Jake".

Jake looks at me. "I'm sorry to put this on you, but there is absolutely nothing you can do?"

I sigh "I wish there was, Jake. I've told her what happened to Clarissa, and what happened to me when she died…and it seemed she understood. But now…I don't know Jake. I'm sorry".

Jake shakes his head. "It's not your fault, and it's not fair for me to ask you for help…just because you went through a similar situation".

"Has she talked to Ally lately?"

Jake nods, and then turns to the sink, which he begins to fill with hot water. "Yeah, she's talking to Ally a lot now….which is progress I gotta say. She wouldn't speak to anyone when Daniel first died".

"Jake…."

He turns his head around to me. "Yeah?"

"I don't know if it will help much…"

Jake interrupts "Honestly Nathan, if it can help her, even just a little bit…I'm all ears".

"Well, I go to a sort of support group…Ally comes too, I forgot to mention that I know her...Anyway, the next meeting's tomorrow, if you think it might help Seren, if she went…?"

Jake thinks “You would be there?”

I nod “And Ally as well”.

Jake turns the tap off, and faces me. “One problem: If I mentioned it to Seren, she would instantly deny that she needs help, and refuse to go”.

I think “What if Ally mentioned it to her?”

Jake shrugs “Same thing would happen”.

He then gets an idea “Unless….”

“Unless, what?”

He looks at his phone for a good few seconds, then frowns. This frown is followed by a smile.

“Nothing, Nathan. Don’t worry about it…You mind giving me a hand with washing up?”

(32) Daniel

I'm still here. Seren interrupted the frequency, but she just knocked me back, though the 'thin white sheet'. And I wasn't able to get back in. And I can still can't. I've fought and reached out. But it won't work. So I'm trapped. I can't go anywhere.

I'm starting to realise that she's always going to blame herself. And that's sounds about right. She believes the impossible, and tries to achieve the impossible.

Even though she believes in Science. I guess she believes that Science is what achieves the impossible.

She's also stubborn. Once she feels and believes something, she'll believe it, and argue it, until she has an *excellent* reason to believe a contradictory statement or feeling.

Once she has that excellent reason, she will accept it instantly. She will let go. But she's not letting herself become open to anything. She wants to believe that it's all her fault. When it isn't.

It was never her fault.

So I'm not giving in. I'm going to fight and reach out, so I can somehow get to her. I'm not going to let her believe it. I'm not going until she realises that it was not her fault.

Once she can accept that it wasn't her fault, then she can move on. And for God's sake, she needs that most of all.

Maybe I can make a hole in this thin white sheet, and find a way to get to her. Either way, I'm going to fight my way through somehow.

I need to reach her somehow. I need her to listen to me. She used to.

(33) Seren.

So, now I'm back to where I started. I'm back on the treadmill, running hard, not wanting to think. He's still not coming. I sent him away twice. And now there won't be a third.

He still has to be here. There's a part of me, about half of me that still hopes that. Until I know otherwise, I will always hope.

But, now, I don't want to think about Daniel. I'm still not talking to Lily. Jake and Mum have talked to her, told her to be a little bit more tactful but it doesn't matter. I can't face her.

So, yeah. My life.

Jake's' still being my big brother. But he's got other priorities. Ally's still being my best friend. But we all know that I'm back at square one.

"Why are we here?" I ask, as Ally weaves and drags me though the busy streets.

"Because you are turning into an Insomniac, and I'm bored," Ally says without turning around.

"So, you came out of the most boring place ever, you're lucky to be alive, and you're...bored?" I say, with raised eyebrows.
She turns around, pretends to think, and nods, with a grin. And then continues to drag me though.

About 10 minutes later, we stop in front of a community building. The walls are just ordinary brick, and the door is an average brown.

“We need to go in here for a bit”.

I frown “Why exactly?”

She starts going up the steps “I need to show you something”.

“Like what?”

She notices I haven’t moved, and comes back down.

“Just trust me okay. If you don’t like it, we can leave...okay?”

I trust Ally completely. So I follow her up the steps into the building. Ally knows this place somehow. She walks through confidently, and doesn’t get confused by the all the turns and corridors.

Ally soon opens a small blue door, and holds it open. I follow her inside to a relatively small room. It’s full of windows, which make it seem larger than it actually is.

A group of comfortable-looking multi-coloured chairs are arranged in a circle. And sitting in one of them, looking a little awkward is Nathan. He looks up as we enter, and smiles, surprised.

I realise where we are now, and begin to walk away, angry. Is this meant to help me? How will it? It'll just trigger memories I can't think about.

Ally grabs my wrist before I can go. I try and get free, but Ally's stronger than she looks. She faces me "You said you would give it a try!"

"No, I didn't. *You* said if I didn't like it, we could go!"

Ally laughs "You haven't given it a try - how can you know if you won't like it or not?"

"You really think I'm going to like a bloody support group? - it's not going to help!"

Ally sighs "Then what will?"

And I can't answer.

She looks at me, and I now she's not lying when she talks again "Listen, it's not like what you think it is- it's not cliché or anything. I started coming here, after I was first diagnosed. It kinda helps. Really. Look, just come and listen. You don't need to talk or anything. Just...try".

I notice she's released the grip on my wrist. "You don't understand" I whisper. It'll just make it real again. The whole accident.

I don't say it, but Ally knows what I'm thinking.

"Thing is, Seren. It *was* real, and we all have to face reality sooner or later. We can't run forever. And running will never solve your problems. It all comes back".

I nod "I know". Because I do. I really do. But running is easier sometimes. And yet, sometimes you have to stop, and let yourself breathe.

We walk to the centre of the room, where Nathan sits. We take two chairs next to him.

He nods at Ally "Hi - haven't seen you for a while".

I look at him surprised "You know each other?"

Ally nods "Hmm, yeah. Remember, when we tried to do the...thing? Besides, Nathan comes every few weeks. I've known him for a couple of months. Should of realised you knew him - he said he was friends with Jake".

Nathan smiles "Actually, I only met Seren a couple of days ago". He turns his attention to me.

"It's good to see you here. It must have been hard".

I nod "Well, I didn't know I was coming. Ally tricked me".

He laughs softly "I can imagine that".

Ally joins in.

And so do I, just a little bit.

And it's not as bad as I thought it would be. A girl opposite us stands up and begins her story "So…Uh...um….Well, I've got Depression." She stops, swallows and carries on. "It's weird. I mean, it's not like being sad all the time…and I can't just be happy. It's like I have no feelings. Some days, I don't even want to get up. I just want to sleep, and forget about all the headaches, and the pain… But I do. It's been three years since I was diagnosed, and I still get so many of those days. And my brother just looks at me, like: Snap out of it, why don't you! You're not sick, you're just trying to get attention! But I'm really not. I can't help it. I would give anything to feel normal again. But I don't. I'm on medication and everything…But it's going to be a while, they say. So, most days, I wish I could just curl up, and never wake up. Cos I don't want to face the world anymore. Some days, I wish I could end it all. But I don't. I carry on fighting. And I wish I could stop. But I can't stop my depression. And now I can't stop fighting. And you know what? I'm glad I can't stop that. I want to continue fighting. I don't want to give in. Every day, I fight though, I'm one day closer to the finishing line - where my depression stops, and I can get off my meds. And that's stronger than any mental illness".

There's a stunned silence. The girl- Kate, I think her name is, sits down, looking slightly embarrassed. A boy, next to Ally reaches across, and says "Tell your brother that he's a complete arse".

Ally has to wait, to let the laugher subside, then she sighs and stands up.

"I was diagnosed with Leukemia, when I was thirteen...so three years ago, or near about. We were told by this doctor, that I might be okay. *Might* be okay. Meanwhile, as he dropped this big bombshell on us, all I could focus on was a picture of a healthy, happy, girl about sixteen - his daughter I think, that he had placed on his desk. And it was like, that girl is what I will probably never be. Even if I survive, my body will be forever changed....The doctor guy caught me looking, and put the photo away, and looked at me in mistrust like he was scared I would pass it over to her. That made me angry... and he looked at us, like 'what are you still doing here?' He didn't even seem to care, that he had dropped something huge on us... That wasn't the worst part of it. I could cope with losing my hair - I did one of those charity head shaves. I figured I was going to lose it anyway - this way, it was kinda my own terms. The chemotherapy changed my body, and made me even sicker. But for me, the worst part was sitting in a crowded waiting room, surrounded by people-most of them my age, and knowing in a couple of years, more than half of them could be dead. I didn't want to give in. But when I was moved to intensive care, I started to wonder. One day, I felt.... I thought it was time. So, I called my best friend".

(She indicates me) “I wanted to say goodbye. Then I don’t remember anymore. I woke up later, and my parents were laughing and crying. I had survived. Somehow. It wasn’t until later that I realised Seren wasn’t there. I asked why. It had been a day since I had called her, and only then did they tell me the truth. That Seren’s boyfriend Daniel, had died. Died. Saving Seren. And then I understood. Someone had to die. And it should have been me. But it wasn’t. It was Daniel. And I feel so selfish, and so guilty. It should have been me. Not him. And Seren blames herself, which makes me feel even worse! It’s my fault. I was ready to die. But Daniel wasn’t. He should have a life.... But now he doesn’t. And I do. And even though it’s tough, I need to accept that, at the end of the day, I’m living. And I should honour that. I’ll remember Daniel, by living the life that he died to give me. I’m going to make my life, the best it can be - for Daniel”.

Ally sits down, slightly breathless. And I realise that’s I’m staring at her in amazement. And I also realise that the rest of the group is trying not to look at me, but know want to hear what I have to say.

Please, no. I’m not ready. I can’t talk about it like Ally and Kate can. Please no...no....no...

Nathan nudges me. “What was Daniel like, Seren?”

I shot him a grateful look. I can talk about that. I think I can. I couldn’t alone. But here...

I look at Nathan...He nods encouragingly. And so does Ally.

"Um...Daniel was" I start and falter. But the group is patient.

"He was...incredible. He liked sport, mostly, but also was reasonably academic - he preferred learning facts, rather than theories, so he hated Phil and Ethics, tolerated Science, but enjoyed History. He didn't really see the point of questioning things we couldn't change or understand. He was about as opinionated as I am-we could debate for hours." I stop for a moment, not sure if I can carry on.

"Go on - you're doing great!" whispers Nathan.

I take a deep breath. "He didn't like video games - thought they were pointless and stupid. His parents were friends with my mum, so I saw him sometimes. But it wasn't until my little sister was born, that we actually paid attention to each other. He smiled at me... I was nine. We began to become quite good friends, - we would go to the park with Jake and Ally, - you know, Kid stuff. I was thirteen when we began to get even closer. We didn't flirt or anything. I was too shy, he was too self-conscious. When we were fourteen, I helped him revise for a mock test in Science. I was better at Science than he...was. Anyway, we both passed with A*'s. We were laughing, caught in the moment... but he pulled me into a hug, and then...just kissed me. And I didn't even realise, but I was kissing him back. And I never even knew how it would feel, but nothing else was important anymore. It was me and him. For our first date, we went to see a Shakespeare play – 'The Tempest' at the theatre. He wouldn't let me see the tickets once - I think they were quite expensive. But he knew I would love the play".

"...He even managed to sneak us into the hospital to see Ally, after she was placed into intensive care. Now that was fun... and kind of stupid. But fun, and totally worth it".

"...Daniel was just...Daniel. But for me...there was nothing else he needed to be. He had green eyes that grinned with mischief, fun and seriousness, all at once. I loved him. I did. And I know, when people our age say they are in love, everyone thinks they're just melodramatic, and stupid, and hormonal. Or it's just puppy love. But it was never that. I loved him. Simple as. And he loved me too".

"I used to ask him why he did. Daniel could have had anyone...but he wanted me. I never understood why. Daniel would laugh, but never give me an answer... He used to ask me the same thing, but then would break off, saying he didn't want an answer. He said the fact that I loved him was enough..."

I break off, I can't talk anymore. I realise I'm shaking, and probably about to start crying. Ally's looking at me in pure amazement, like she couldn't believe I actually would. "Well done...."

I turn to the right of me where Nathan's smiling. I look at him, still shaking.

"Hey" he whispers "You did great. You did well for one day".

It's then I realise that Nathan's holding my hand. And he continues holding it until I stop shaking.

And I realise how much I missed someone holding my hand like that. It feels good, and great, and brilliant.

And now I realise that I'm actually crying. But it's okay. It's safe to cry here. No one will judge you for it. Or think anything about it. Instead, it feels like we all cry together. By telling our stories, we share our emotions, and we let go slightly.

It's easier to run, but sometimes, you need to stop and breathe.

(34) Nathan.

After the support group, myself, Ally and Seren walk home together. Seren and I aren't in particularly talkative moods. But that doesn't matter -Ally is. She talks enough for all three of us.

Seren looks slightly shell-shocked. But she's able to walk and says she feels fine. Ally and I knew she was lying when she said that. At which point, Ally flashes me a quick look, and it's settled. I'm walking back with them.

I've never heard Seren talk like that, let alone about Daniel. I didn't even realise I was holding her hand, and I don't know for how long I was. I think I reached out when she started to falter, but I don't know when she held on.

I could say she reminded me of Clarissa, but that would be a lie. I never held Clarissa's hand like that - to give her support. Rissa never needed support. She did use to talk like that though. Start of slowly, then gather speed, as she gradually forget where she was, and got into whatever topic she was thinking about the present moment. I see Clarissa in her sometimes, but most of the time, I see Clarissa in almost everything.

Ally laughs and chats, but I notice she keeps giving little glances over to Seren. She looks amazed - like she's surprised that Seren actually *spoke,* a little bit satisfied, and the rest of her looks damm well pleased with herself. Well, she got her there, I guess. Who would have thought that it would actually work? She also looks a little concerned, but not completely panicked- which is a little reassuring.

Seren looks up at me, and gives a small, shy smile. She gradually seems to be coming back to normal. She's drawing back into herself again though. But that's okay. Small steps. She spoke aloud about Daniel - that's progress. It's doing fine. Small, tiny steps. For Seren, it seems to be the best way forward.

"Well, this is me" says Ally, breaking my thoughts. Seren looks startled as well. But it's true. We are at Ally's house, who hugs her best friend, and yells "See you next week, Nathan!" as she walks up the steps leading to her front door.

And now it's just Seren and me. Right. Slightly awkward. She's Jake's younger sister after all...

Seren looks unsure "Um...should we go?" And I realise we've been standing outside of Ally's house, for a few minutes.

"Oh Right! Yes...we should".

Seren smiles again, but not in mockery. We start walking slowly down the street.

"What was Clarissa like?" she asks suddenly. I look at her sharply and in surprise.

She looks down at her feet "I'm sorry. I didn't mean to be untactful...I mean, you don't have to answer...it's just..."

“Oh, no…it’s fine” I say quickly and it kind of is - sort of. It feels kind of right, telling Seren. She’s one of the few people that knows the full story of Clarissa’s death. The others, being her parents, my own parents and my counsellor. I’ve spoken about what Clarissa was like, during support group, but not the whole story. With Seren, it’s different.

I think for a few minutes “Clarissa had blonde, curly hair, and green eyes that always were wide open - she wanted to know and see more. She was tall - about the same height as me. She was always questioning everything about the world, and wondering about faith, culture…anything. So, her favourite topic was Phil and Ethics. She liked Science as well - but she preferred *why* the world works, over *how* the world works. She was obsessed with the stars - she was always wondering, what they could symbolise-I never knew what she saw in them, that was fascinating. She liked astrology, and astronomy, but didn’t particularly believe in Horoscopes. Now *that* I understood. I know she sounds quite eccentric, but she was actually quite down to earth. Quite focused. Serious. She did have a good sense of humour though. She loved reading, and writing. She was very imaginative - she loved English. She disliked her teacher though - apparently she was too old school, no imagination. She was independent - like she never needed anyone to support her. She was quite logical. Very sensible. I rarely heard her swear, she didn’t do any stupid things - like Ally would”.

Seren laughs at that.

"Um...She never actually *hated* anyone. There would be a few people she disliked, but she could never say she hated anyone - it wasn't in her nature. She had an answer for everything. If she didn't know, she would think about it for the next few hours. She found everything fascinating. God, I found her fascinating. She was different, so unique, and the only person that could understand Calculus like I do".

Seren laughs again, and she's lost her shell- shocked look. She's back to normal. I look at her.

"Does that answer your question?"

She nods slowly "Yes it did".

I notice we're outside her house. And she notices as well, and sighs quietly.

She looks uncomfortable "Do you want to come in?...Jake's here".

I probably look uncomfortable as well "Oh, I better be headed home...got revision."

"Calculus?" She quips.

I laugh "Nope, finished that last week".

She laughs too.

And we're back to awkward silence.

She smiles, at nothing it seems.

"...Thank you, Nathan, for everything today".

I look at her "Seren...it was a pleasure".

She smiles fully- a proper smile. And I realise it's the first time I've seen her smile like that.

"See you later Nathan".

"See you soon Seren".

And before it can get even more awkward, Seren turns around, and runs to her front door. As she opens it, she looks at me again, and smiles again, just before the door shuts.

And I'm left standing there, not knowing what to think. I look at the door for a few seconds, then turn around and head for home, fully aware of the grin that stretches across my face, making me look like that cat from Alice in wonderland. *We're all mad here.* Yes, we all are.

(35) Seren.

I shut the door, and collapse against it. I start laughing, which makes me start to cry. But it feels different this time. I continue crying, but I also carry on laughing. And it's weird.

I'm probably making some really strange noises, so it's no wonder that Jake runs out, probably wondering which one of his sisters has strangled the other one.

He sees me, still collapsed against the door, and immediately kneels down.

"Seren? I think you might be in shock."

I start laughing even harder. Because of how serious he's taking it. And how my version of shock, involves me laughing.

But all he sees is me crying even harder, and making some even stranger noises.

"Seren, take a deep breath."
Because he does know what he is doing, I listen to him, and draw in a slow hiccupping breath. And laugh again.

"Seren! Keep taking in deep breaths....That's it....that's good....okay".

I'm finally back to normal. "Thanks Jake".

He frowns at me "What happened? How does going out with Ally get you into shock?"

"...Um...she tricked me into going to a..."

He stares at me "Does the words 'support group' finish that sentence?"

"Um...yep".

He gets up, and extends a hand to get me up.

"Thought it might. Nathan goes to one today - did you see him?"

This lets loose another load of laughing. Jake looks at me, slightly wary. "Oh, yes. I *definitely* saw him."

Jake assesses me to make sure I'm not going into shock again. Then rolls his eyes.

"Women" he mutters.

I laugh, and head upstairs.

I don't quite know how I feel. I really don't. I feel a little bit shell-shocked, a little bit hyper, and little bit crazy. And part of me still feels blank. But it's not all of me, and less of me than it usually is.

I never thought I could even say all I did today. And it did help. It took the edge away. And it helped knowing you're not along. That they won't judge you if you start going hysterical. But they're judge if they know what I did...

When speaking at the group, and talking to Nathan, the guilt I felt subsided. But now I'm alone. And it starts to come back. Slowly. But steadily.

Nathan was the one that really helped today. He gave me his hand, and lent me support, without even saying a word.

A part of my mind, thinks, "Could I have done it without Nathan or Ally being there?"

And I already know part of the answer.

If no one I knew was there, then no way.

If it had only been Ally, I would definitely have spoken. She was the one that took me, after all. Maybe she helped the most-she always does.

But, my mind persists, if it had only been Nathan, would you have spoken as much then?

And I know the answer. I really do.

But it doesn't matter. They were both there. They both helped in their own way. And I spoke about Daniel. About what he was like. And it hurt so much. And yet, when I carried on, the pain receded. Instead of drowning, with my head trapped underwater. I lifted it up. I breathed. I was alive again.

My gaze shifts to my laptop that buzzes on my desk. I think about it, and decide I haven't felt this mentally strong for a while. And who knows when I will again?

I sit down, and lift the screen up. Type in the password, and navigate to Google. Without thinking, I type in the website name. Facebook.

The first thing I see, is the notification buttons. Showing I have many unread messages, and many notifications.

I haven't been on this site for a while. I wanted to isolate myself. And I still want too. But that's not why I'm here.

I type in Daniel Luccan in the search bar, and click on the first icon I see.

The first thing I see is all the notifications.

My god… Why you mate?

Daniel… you will be missed so f*cking much…

Please tell me it's some kind of horrible joke…

I close my eyes for a second, so I won't have to see. And think about what I need to see. I open my eyes, avert them, and click on 'Photos'.

And like I kind of hoped it wouldn't be, the first picture is of me and him outside the theatre, when we saw 'The Tempest'. .

I smile anyway. The picture's crap, as we hadn't quite got the hang of selfies yet, and his thumb is partially in the way. And we aren't actually looking at the phone either. But it's not completely crap. It's kind of perfect...in a crap way.

I click the next one. A picture of the football team he played in. He, as man of the match, sits in the middle, balancing the trophy. He's muddy, exhausted, bright red, but he's laughing. He looks... I can't describe it. But my memories still do him justice.

The next one. Him and me again. The next one. Him, Ally, Jake and myself, at some kind of party I can't even remember. Moving on. Him, and some couple of classmates, being fourteen year olds.

I click though all the photos, there's not many. But it's something I needed to see. Daniel. As he was.

I exit the photos, and scroll down to his last status. It takes a long time. I have to go through all the messages left. I could simply go on to my own profile. But I haven't been on Facebook, since it happened. And I don't want to see the messages left on my profile-my relationship with Daniel was no secret. I don't want to see my friends living their life - I can't enter my own life just yet.

Eventually I get there. His many status updates. What he shared on. And one of them is a charity advert about cancer. Actually most of them are.

I carry on, and read them all. Take my time. Some make me laugh, and others make me cry. It shows Daniel living his life, just like any other normal teenager. Only, he wasn't normal to me.

I loved him, and....I still do. I always will.

And I don't deserve to still love him. How can I? I'm responsible for his death, yet I love him, in my crazy, stupid, guilt ridden body.

I've had enough now, and I've reached the end of all he ever shared and wrote. I begin to shut down Facebook, when I see the icons showing who's online, and ready to chat. By some coincidence, most of the people who I called my friends can chat.

I don't even realise, that my mouse has sent the cursor over there, where it hovers, shaking and deliberating.

I'm tempted, I really am. I almost click on one of the names. When I sent the cursor to the right hand corner, and close down the website. I then shut the laptop, with more force than I actually intended.

I lean with my head on my desk, realising that I'm bone tired, and completely exhausted. I wasn't ready. I can't talk to anyone else yet. I don't deserve to. I'm not ready....I'll never be ready.... I'm a murderer.

Something falls from one of the shelves I have around my bedroom. I watch it fall, and remember.

When I was 14, for my birthday, Daniel brought me a book - one I had wanted for a while. He then took me to see a film at the cinema, and we help hands all the way through it. For my 15th birthday, he took me to a posh, upmarket restaurant, and brought me a bracelet, from an expensive shop. When I turned sixteen, he took me to see a film, then we went to an even more upmarket, and even more posh restaurant. Outside, snow was falling, and the stars shone though. He then told me he loved me, and I said the same back to him.

He then passed over a small box. I opened it slowly, and revealed a small, tiny and perfect crystal, shaped into a star. It captured the light, and cast rainbow patterns everywhere. I didn't know what to say-but I think my face captured what I was feeling. Daniel laughed, said he had a job and bank account, was happy that I loved it, and no, he would never tell me how much it cost.

And I can never fully describe how much I loved him at that moment.

And now, the crystal star has fallen from my shelf, and is now lying on the floor in my bedroom. And yet, it hasn't broken. I lean over and pick it up, where it nestles in the palm of my hand, reflecting rainbows over my bedroom.

But it's cold, and harsh, and perfect - like that day. Now, it seems too perfect. Because nothing will be like that day again. The coldness and the harshness, show nothing of the perfect memories, it should represent.

I want to throw it, and break it. So it shows what perfect turns into to. But something stops me...It was the last thing Daniel brought for me.

I slowly get up, and look around for a place where I won't have to look at it. So I walk over to a shelf, where I can place it behind a huge ornament. But I stop and look at it. And start thinking. Why did this crystal, of all the ornaments I own fall at this point. Why now, when I was thinking of Daniel, and the crystal. What caused this to fall, when everything else is undisturbed? Why this, why now? Almost like someone has pushed it. Someone invisible.... Daniel. Is he here?

I close my eyes, realising the star is still in my hand. I clutch at it desperately. I try to let my mind go blank. I'm tired. So tired. I try to let my mind open up. The silence inside my bedroom is suffocating.

It may be my imagination, my exhaustion. But I think I can feel a *presence.* Something I can't explain, but part of it is realising you're not alone. I shut my eyes tighter, if that was even possible. Inside my head, I *reach out,* try to expand my mind out from the regions it resides in.

But then my exhaustion kicks in. No sound is oppressive. No sight is oppressive. I have to open my eyes. I don't want too. I try to keep them shut. I really do. But like an impulse, my eyes fly open. Leaving me back in my room, reality. Like the presence I felt never existed. But I know it did.

I look at the star again, and place in behind the tall ornament. That way I won't have to see it.

(36) Nathan.

I look at the night sky one more time, sigh and slip back into my bedroom. Still no meteor shower. Like there ever would be.

I needed to see one. I wanted to. It was important tonight. Because in the two years since she left, I spoke to someone who matters as much as she did. And I told someone more than I have ever told anyone else.

So, I needed to remind myself of Clarissa. If I had seen a meteor shower....I could remember what it felt like to be with her. I could have finally said goodbye. Let go.

Seren's different from Clarissa, but also the same. When I was with Clarissa, being with her felt....right. Like we blended around each other. She was calm, and collected. It felt surreal as well - it didn't feel like reality. She was like a never ending starry night sky.

When I look at Seren...sparks fly. She's passionate, and also an emotional wreck. She's a meteorite. Stunning, passionate, fiery. It feels rare, but not unnatural. When I look at her, I feel hot - like she's a flame that never goes out. And that flame doesn't shine as bright as she should.

She's incredible.

For me, you just can't not look at her. She takes my attention, and my breath away.

For others, she's light. She could avoid being noticed. She could blend in. But not blend with me, like Clarissa could.

With Clarissa, colours merged, stars shone. We went together naturally.

With Seren, colours break out, stars flame. We aren't unnatural.

I realise I'm grinning stupidly again. Just the thought of her makes me laugh, like I've just received the most shocking, but brilliant news, in all of history.

Of course, I still feel guilt and uneasiness. The thought of Clarissa still takes me. I think of her all the time.

I loved her. And I always will. But now, a meteorite falls. This meteorite begins to take my attention as she burns herself out. This meteorite needs to get back up again, become a meteor instead.

The closer I get to her, the more I burn, the more I flame with her. The less I think of Clarissa.

But I never said goodbye. She hangs over me.

One day, I may not even think of her at all. And that can never happen. How can I let it happen in good conscience - after all that happened? How can you turn your back on the starry sky, and never see the stars again?

But how can you turn your attention away from a meteorite?

And the thing about Meteorites. They don't last. They burn out. And what if I lose Seren, like I lost Clarissa?

She has her gold hair arranged up in a top knot, and her emerald eyes are half shut in concentration. She knows I'm listening, which makes her even more nervous. Her hands, painted with light blue nail polish hold the bow so carefully and gently, and bring it across her violin with perfect precision. She's playing a song I have heard before, but it's beautiful.

We're in the study at her house. I'm sitting at the desk, supposed to be making my way through a set of questions on Calculus whilst Clarissa practices her violin. Even though Calculus is one of my favourite subjects, Clarissa is much more memorising. For obvious, clear reasons.

mesmorising

With a flourish, she brings the bow across the last string. She waits until the music dies before taking away the bow, and bringing the violin down from her collarbone. She turns to me with a smile.

"What did you think?" she asks whilst carefully placing the violin back in its green case. As green as her eyes, I think drowsily, before realising she's asked me a question.

I wake up, and meet her inquiring, gentle eyes.

"It was...beautiful" I tell her honestly. "You've got a real talent".

She smiles again, and ducks her head in modesty. Her hair is starting to come loose, and strands cover her face.

"I've never heard anything like that before, Rissa. What was it?"

She lifts her hand up and releases the hair still gathered up. "It was originally a tribal song I heard whilst growing up in South Africa. I think it belongs to the Zulu tribe. I thought I would try and see if I could play it on the violin, once I got good enough. I'm surprised I actually remembered it.

Her hair flows down her back, and almost reaches her waist.

"I didn't realise you could play tribal songs on a violin".

She laughs ."Neither did I".

"How long were you living in South Africa?"

Rissa puts her head on one side and thinks for a moment. "It must have been about seven years. Callum and I were born there. Our parents, being diplomats, were doing some kind of job there. So, when we were seven, I think, we moved to Italy for a month or so, as mum was offered a job there. We stayed with some relatives. Then Dad was given a job in Greece, so we moved there, and managed to meet some distant relatives. We were there for a year. Dad was given a job in Britain, and Mum wanted to give work up, so we settled in London, and eventually moved down here".

She continues to place her violin away and I look at her in wonder. "You have had the most amazing life".

She smiles at me. "It's still going on. I hope it becomes even more amazing".

"...So you're South African, Italian, Greek, and British?" I ask.

She laughs again. "Not quite. I'm mostly British. I'm only about a quarter Italian, and less than a quarter Greek. The rest of me is completely British".

I shake my head slowly and smile. "I'm boring compared to you".

She looks at me curiously. "How so?"

"I'm completely British. No interesting blood".

She shakes her head, also smiling. "On the contrary, I think British blood is very interesting".

She glances up at the large skylight placed in the ceiling.

If even possible, her smile becomes even broader.

"The stars are out" she says gesturing. I stand up, and come to stand next to her.

I gaze up. Sometimes, I can see why Clarissa loves stars.

So, I get an idea.

"Shall we get a closer look?"

(37) Seren.

I know he's still here. I just can't reach him. Or maybe he doesn't want to reach out to me....Maybe he finally begins to blame me. It's selfish and stupid. But I want him to blame me. I need him to blame me. I need him to accept what I am. What I truly am. But the selfish part is that I still want him to stay. I want him to never leave. What will happen if he leaves - really goes? I'll forget him. And I'll forget the guilt. I'll forget what I did. I'll accept what I did. But I can't. I can't forget this.

Maybe he saw Nathan. Maybe he got the wrong idea.

It's easy to. But Nathan's just a friend. A good friend. He shouldn't even my friend. He's Jake's friend. Not mine.

But...he is. I think he is. I don't know. But how can he be? How can he be something more? I'm scared he is.

I have to stay away from him. I can't be near him. I can't let another person near me. Because I don't deserve this, after what I did to Daniel.

I'm scared of letting someone near me again.

I can't let someone near me again.

All I could focus on is what happened to the last person I loved. And what I did to the last person I loved.

Nathan's different from Daniel. In many ways. And yet, though I try to deny and hide it, I think I'm beginning to feel the same way I felt about Daniel.

But I can't. I have to choke it down, and wait for it to recede. Because it has to.

Daniel was the first, and last person I can ever love. And I can't even think about him. I don't the right to even remember him as I do. I can't think about Daniel.

Or Nathan.

I need to distract myself, keep my mind busy.

But now, looking around my room. all I can see is memories.

Photos.

Places he sat. Places he stood.

The text book we looked at.

The book he brought me.

Books he touched.

Films we watched together.

An iPod, full of music we listened to.

The speakers where the music we chose sung out.

The floor where he pulled me, and we danced.

Key rings we got from every place we ever went to.

The microscope where we freaked each other out.

The mini IQ test we took for a joke.

The desk, where we did our homework together.

The phone we texted each other with.

The tickets to the first place we went to together.

I walk down the stairs slowly. The hallway where we fell, soaking wet, laughing, after getting caught in the rain.

The kitchen, where we made hot chocolate, with extra marshmallows, whipped cream, and a flake.

The garden where we read together, and we got sprayed by a water hose.

The dining room, where Daniel first ate with my family.

The living room where Lily quizzed us about…'adult stuff'.

My mind circles around, and around. It buzzes, and screams inside of me. I have a headache.

I can't breathe.

"Seren?"

I blink. It's gone. My mind still buzzes and still screams. I look up at where Jake should be sitting. Where Lily should be watching cartoons.

But no-one's there.

My mind's hard to ignore. It moves faster than my body can.

I walk over to a room, and open the door.

A treadmill waits.

I slam the door with more force than I intended.

(38) Nathan.

I don't know why I'm doing this. I really don't. But somehow, I think I need too.

But why now? I think I know why too.

Because now is the time I'm scared of letting go. Now is the time, I'm wondering how to let go. Because I never really have.

So, I get on my bike, and ride slowly down familiar and unfamiliar streets.

The wind hits me and it hurts.

But I don't mind.

It can never hurt as much as other things do.

Rissa came into my life like she belonged in it. She came in like a missing piece that I didn't even know was missing. She came in quickly. She also left quickly.

I first met her in a Philosophy and Ethics class. It was fifth period, just after lunch. Because of that, most of us always came in late.

I needed to calm down. I was trying to stop taking it – the stuff I kept poisoning my lungs with. I wanted to stop.

So I decided to go to my class about five minutes early. I thought that getting into class would get me into a 'concentrating' mood and I would calm down. I would stop fidgeting, and be able to focus on something.

I was also looking for solitude. I was embarrassed for people to see me in the state I was in.

So I almost ran to the classroom, and opened the door, expecting to see an empty classroom which is exactly what I wanted.

But of course I didn't.

I opened the door, and thrust myself in, breathing deeply.

To find a girl I had never seen before sitting there by herself, writing in a book.

She had gold hair that was long and looked like it was illuminated like a million tiny lights.

She looked up as I entered, and studied me curiously. She smiled, and nodded at me, acknowledging me.

Her eyes are green, I remember thinking, in a daze. They were intuitive, like she could know everything about you.

But she never would. And she would never judge. She would understand.

And I realised, the minute I saw her, that was exactly what I wanted. To be understood, without being judged.

I didn't even know her name - she was new.

I sat down on the other side of the classroom, pretending to get things out, but all the time, I tried not to study her.

Which of course I did.

She seemed different, which she was.

Even the light around her seemed different.

Like small invisible particles of light were dancing and whirling around her.

She looked like light was part of her. That it belonged to her.

That she couldn't be real. But of course, she was.

It was probably only a minute, but it felt like hours.

It felt like electricity, like lightening.

The mystery girl studied me, when she thought I couldn't see.

I did the same.

And one time, our eyes met.

But we didn't look away. It was like we couldn't.

Even her eyes were full of light.

She was the one that spoke first.

"I'm Clarissa". Her voice was gentle, but with a strange lilt. It was full of stars, and light. It had connotations of wisdom, of philosophy.

She looked at me, with a smile, and I realised I hadn't spoken.

"Oh! I'm Nathan".

Her smile grew broader, if that was even possible.

And that was it. It had begun.

For more than a year, I had inhaled substances with strange narcotics in an attempt to feel something, anything.

It was never enough. I either never found what I was looking for, or I had a small grasp of it, but I could never hold on to it, or it was only a small pretence of something bigger.

And after so long I had finally found it. In Clarissa. I never even thought that I ever would.

I would like to say that I stopped taking drugs at that point. And I can honestly say that, I did slow down. It was easier to resist.

But, I took those drugs, not realising or thinking about what I was putting in my body. But I knew now. Addiction.

I was getting better, but I wasn't fixed.

I never told Rissa, but somehow she knew.

And she never judged.

She encouraged me with her smile, and eyes, full of light. They said everything I wanted but also needed to hear.

They said I could fight the cravings, and become stronger.

And sometimes I believed it.

She was a mystery. I never fully understood her. But I didn't mind. She understood me.

I loved her. I think she loved me. That was enough. More than enough.

We once took our bikes to a National Trust park in the middle of night, in the middle of summer.

And the stars shone bright.

She told me their names, and the constellations they made.

I told her legends and stories of what people believed the stars were.

She told me her own.

I told her facts and figures.

We talked about everything that mattered, and everything that didn't.

I didn't even realise that she was gently grasping my hand, and I gently grasped hers.

And I didn't know what my life would be without Clarissa.

And she said, with her eyes and voice, that she didn't know what her life would be without me.

So, we promised each other, we would never find out.

We would leave the world together, and start the next chapter with each other.

And I promised myself that I would get better. I would force myself to get myself off the things I forced into my body.

I would stop.

I would stop.

But it wasn't until Rissa died, that I actually did.

I look around confused. I have no idea, where the hell I am.

It's been a while, but how can I forget something like that?

How can I?

I'm lost. In more ways than one.

Time moves on, and it takes our memories with it, Clarissa would say.

But it moves too fast. And our memories come too slow.

I find the right way eventually, and come up to the right house.

I get off my bike, and walk slowly up the path.

I stare at the door for a few minutes. Then carry on walking.

I can't give in.

But I know it's going to take all my strength and resolve to open that door.

As it turns out, I don't have too.

The door swings open.

For a minute, I expect to see Clarissa standing there.

But instead, it's her twin brother, Callum.

He starts off smiling, then recognises me. His smile freezes, and becomes confused. His eyebrows raise, as I walk up to him.

He speaks first.

"Well, I guess you should come in".

He turns around, not waiting to see if I will follow. But he's not an idiot. He knows I will.

So, now we sit in the living room, holding steaming mugs of coffee that Callum made.

Surrounding us, are many, many photos. Most of time are of Clarissa and Cal growing up.

We haven't spoken since Callum offered to make the coffee.

He stares at me in obvious disbelief.

"Why now?" he finally says. "You haven't been over, since she...died. I haven't seen or heard of you, since the funeral!"

I nod. "I know..."

He continues. "We wanted to see you, Nathan. We knew you needed help! We knew you blamed yourself".

I look, confused, at him. "Wait..."

"No, Nathan...we never blamed you! We knew you loved her! You would never harm her!"

I let that sink in.

"I wanted to come, and see you guys...but I couldn't. How could I? Every time, it just got harder, Cal. I got to the door once, then I just left. I couldn't face it..."

Cal shakes his head. "Yeah, we should have realised that...we knew what you were like!"

We both laugh. It's not funny, but it's all we can do.

Cal takes a sip of his coffee. "So then…like I said, why now?"

I don't really know what to say. Cal studies me, and nods to himself. He has Rissa's talent for intuitiveness.

"Right" he says.

He takes another sip. "She loved you a lot, you know".

I look at him, and he continues.

"You meant everything to her...believe me, she was my twin, and for me, her face was an open book!"

He smiles. "She would smile every time she heard your name. You could tell she was thinking about you…her whole face would look happy".

I look at him "How…Just how can you talk about her….so easily?"

I may have learnt to start to move on, but I can never talk about Rissa, like Cal does.

He sighs. "Because you have too. Because, talking about her keeps her memory. It keeps her alive within you. Because, speaking about her reminds you that she lived, that she was part of our lives. Because, we can remember who she was, and we can remember the time we had with her. It means it wasn't for nothing. It means we can tell everyone who will listen, that we know that will happen next, that we aren't afraid, but we aren't ready either! It shows that she is still here, that we won't forget her, and the time she was alive! It lets us move on, Nate, and it lets us live!"

I look at Cal with new respect. He was close to his sister, and he's stronger than I am.

He looks seriously at me.

"By not speaking about her, you deny her existence. And, you also deny yourself a life. You become overwhelmed, and full of guilt. Nate, when Rissa died, we all felt guilt, but believe me, we never blamed you. Listen to me now, at first it hurts like everything when you let yourself finally speak about her. You're living and she's not. But that pain you feel is life! You are alive, Nathan, and yes, she's not! But you are! And life is not about numbness or forgetting, it's about anger, and pain, and emotion. And, my sister, your girlfriend, would want you to live! Not just survive, she would want to you feel alive! And love is an emotion, Nate, and she would want you to feel it! In fact, she would want you to feel everything and anything. She would want you to feel the best and worst times of life. Life is a series of emotions, a series of moments, and they all connect. You know it's true, Nathan. I know you do".

I look at him, and I know he's right.

So, I take a deep breath. "Do you remember that time when she brought that camera, and took so many photos?"

Cal laughs. "She used up the whole film in like a day!

He then looks at me. "She did get those photos printed, you know. I had to do it for her - you know what she and computers were like...did you ever see them? -they were good."

I shake my head. "No…no, I didn't."

He makes a gesture with the side of his head. "I think you need too…C'mon".

He leads me up the stairs.

I would know the way to her room blindfolded, but I don't say anything. This is for him, not just for me.

And we come to a closed door. Which we stare at for a few minutes.

"I haven't been in here, since she died". Cal admits "You know what she was like about her room".

I nod "It was more than a bedroom to her. It was like her…her…sanctuary, I guess you could say."

He nods to himself "But she would want us to…go in. Especially now".

He steels himself, and pushes it open.

And we stand in the room of the girl whose life touched us in more ways we can describe.

I don't know what I expect to find.

But it feels full. Like there are memories here that I will never understand.

But it also feels empty. Like the memories have died away and gone with the spirit of the girl they belonged too.

The room is just a room. Four walls, a window. But it's what the room holds, that makes it special, that makes it yours.

That's something she would say.

She would also say, that walls, door and windows hold more secrets than anyone will know.

And now I understand.

The memories of Rissa, which she left on the world will never go. They never do.

Energy is not created or destroyed. That's what Seren would say.

But memories are the energy of life. That's what Rissa would say. And we don't create memories. They come to us, when it is time for us to experience them.

Memories never leave. They remain hidden in everything. It's only the people that go and stop remembering.

(39)Seren.

The three of us laugh, as we walk up the road, to my house. Our ties are loose, top buttons undone, blazers off.

It was our first day of Year 10 today, and Jake's first full week at Sixth form. He had a couple of free periods, so he went home early.

Ally's between treatments, and was judged well enough to go to school with us. That made us all happy. I couldn't imagine going into Year 10 without my best friend.

Daniel's got his arm wrapped around my shoulders, and Ally walks-or practically skips on my other side. She's wearing a beret today - navy and sky blue, the colours of our school.

"She actually tried to make you take it off?" says Daniel within fits of laughter.

Ally nods "Yeah! After Mum called up yesterday and asked for permission for me to wear it because APPARENTLY 'I am extremely self - conscious about having to start Year 10, hairless'. Mum says she was so 'understanding' and 'pleasant' on the phone. But today she was like..." Ally adopts a really posh, weird accent "I don't care what I said to your mother yesterday, Alexa Charlotte Smith. That...*monstrosity* on your head is not school uniform, and I want it off now!"

"So, what happened next?" I ask.

Ally laughs. "Well, I said, so you don't care what you said to my mother yesterday? Then she goes, 'No Alexa, I do not! Now take that thing off!' So, I take the hat off, and just stare at her. And she looks completely horrified. I don't think she actually expected me to be completely bald. Then I realised why she was looking so…terrified".

"And why was she so scared then Ally?" asks Daniel, his body shaking with fits of laughter.

Ally giggles. "Well, do you remember about a week ago, we brought those temporary tattoos?"

Daniel stares at her. "You're telling me the tattoos are still on your scalp?!"

Ally nods slowly, grinning. And we all burst out laughing again.

"Oh god!" I say.. "I arranged the letter tattoos on your forehead, so it would say 'Eff you cancer'!"

Ally's grin goes wider. "Problem was, the 'cancer' part had rubbed off".

Daniel laughs. "What did she do then?"

Ally, still grinning explains. "Well, I sort of bobbed my head forward, so she could see them all. And I'm not kidding, she took two steps backwards. Then I said 'You do realise my mother works for Ofsted, right?' And you could see her face go completely white. And then she says in a really shaky voice, 'Actually I think it will be perfectly fine if you wear the hat after all'. So I put it back on, smile and say 'Thank you Miss. I've got to go to third period now'. And then I just walked past her. I could hear her say "You're...welcome?"

We're still laughing when we walk through the front door into the hallway.

Jake sitting on one of the sofa's in the sitting room hears us.

"What's so funny?"

We all troop into the sitting room, and relay the story back to him.

After during his fair share of laughing, Jake then looks at Ally, who is now lounging in the armchair. Daniel and I are curled up on the opposite sofa to Jake.

"So, which teacher was it?" he asks.

Ally thinks for a second, head on one side "Mrs...Futon? Luton maybe? I don't know. She's quite tall, blonde."

"Oh... Mrs Suton!" Jake says. "I had her for third period. God, no wonder she looked flustered and panicked...should off known it was to do with you, Ally!"

"You really should have" Ally agrees. "What's she like, anyway, will she remember this, hold a grudge?"

Jake frowns "I've only known her for a week, but she seems alright. She doesn't seem like the kind of person that would hold a grudge. She probably won't report it or anything".

Ally nods, satisfied. "That's okay then."

"What about the other new teachers?" I ask "What're they like?"

Jake shrugs. "Name some".

"Mr Reginald?"

Jake makes a face. "Rude…perfectionist, sticks to the rules completely".

"Ms Kaden?" offers Daniel.

Jake thinks for a moment. "Meh".

"Mrs Oona?" Ally asks.

Jake shakes his head "Haven't had her".

Ally sits back disappointed, then thinks of something else.

"Oh, what about Mr Kellan?"

Jake thinks. "Irish".

Daniel leans forward and stares at him. "Hey!"

“You’re only a quarter Irish” Jake counters. “Mr Kellan is 101% Irish”.

Daniel smiles, and settles back on the sofa. He weaves his hand though my mine.

Jake watches us and rolls his eyes.

“You guys got any homework today?”

“Um, I got Maths and Geography” I say.

“Geography and Spanish” groans Daniel.

Ally thinks “Geography and Maths”.

Jake looks at us all, now looking like we belong in a pit of despair.

“Need some help?”

“Oh God, Yes!”

“Absolutely!”

“If you actually can help us, then hell, yes!”

“Wait, did you get homework as well, Jake?”

Jake shakes his head, grinning, as we all stare in annoyance and disbelief.

So, this is why, 10 minutes later, all of us four are sitting at the kitchen table, surrounded by laptops, tablets, textbooks and mugs of hot chocolate with whipped cream (because we needed a sugar hit). We are also surrounded by plates that used to hold crackers, as I casually mentioned that starch, in the long run, provides more energy,

Jake remembered that he actually did have homework - a 2500 word essay, due in on Monday. For about 5 minutes, he was glaring at us, as we were complaining about our homework, which consisted of 1-page worksheets, two tasks on 'MyMaths', and research on types of erosion.

"Jake, what's the answer to Question 6?"

He barely glances at my laptop screen. "42".

"That's the answer to everything" Ally says under her breath.

"Whatever you say, Slartibartfast" responds Daniel.

Ally sends a paper aeroplane towards his head. "Deep thought, Daniel, Deep thought".

I smile. Daniel grins. Ally giggles.

"Enough with the Hitchhiker's Guide to the Galaxy references" Jake groans.

"The second most powerful computer in the universe" I say at the exact same time.

Jake sighs "Don't you start, Seren! – You're meant to be the smart, mature one...when I'm not around, that is".

"Well...you are around, Jake". I point out.

Jake turns his attention back to his laptop. "Jake isn't here, right now. Please leave a message."

"You sound like Marvin the Paranoid Android".

"He sounds nothing like Marvin the Paranoid Android".

"Why is Marvin 'Paranoid'? Isn't he more depressed?"

"Be quiet Daniel, or I'll get Seren to give you another lesson on meteorites.

"Oh, not again!"

"Seren?"

"A shooting star is a Meteor which is a piece of interplanetary matter".

"ARGGGGG".

"Did the Doctor park the Tardis on a meteor?"

"I bet you thought that was really clever".

"Actually yes, I did".

"You know nothing Jon Snow".

"OHHHHH".

"HODOR".

"The Lannisters send their regards".

"HODOR".

"*Dracarys*".

"No, Khaleesi!"

"Valar Morghulis".

"Valar Dohaeris".

"WINTER IS COMING!"

"THE NORTH REMEMBERS!"

"A Lannister pays its debts".

"Stick 'em with the Pointy end".

"For the Watch, Jon Snow".

"When you play the Game of Thrones, you win or die".

"There is no middle ground".

"I'm not threatening the King, I'm educating my nephew".

"YOU'RE TALKING TO A KING!"

"NOW I'VE STRUCK A KING! Did my Hand fall off?"

"Well no, but Jaime's did".

Ally hesitates "What do we say to the God of Death?"

"NOT TODAY!"

Jake slowly lifts his head up from the laptop. "Would you three mind keeping silent for ONE MINUTE! - Are you even ALLOWED to watch Game of Thrones anyway?!"

After glaring at every one of us, he looks down at his laptop and gets on with his essay.

What Jake doesn't know is that we all wearing watches.

So after timing a minute exactly, we all start singing 'Marvin's Lullaby, also from The Hitchhikers guide to the Galaxy.

"Now the world has gone to bed, darkness won't engulf my head. I can see by infrared. How I hate the night. Now I lay me down to sleep, try to count electric sheep. Sweet dream wishes you can keep. How I hate the night".

As we sing, Jake glares at us all. When we finish, we stare innocently back at him.

"Do you lot plan this?" he says exasperated. "Or, just make it up as you go along?"

Daniel shrugs "It's really a mixture of both".

Ally chips in "I mean, we don't actually have much to do when I'm in hospital after all".

Jake nods his head "Hmm...that is very true". He looks down at his watch.

"You guys good to leave your work for later?"

We all nod.

Jake closes down his laptop "Okay, I can finish this tomorrow".

He looks at us all. "Okay, it's Friday...about five. Mum's not home until about nine...Ally, Daniel, how long can you both stay?"

Ally shrugs "Mum's fine with me staying over if I want too".

Daniel checks his phone. "I don't think Mum will mind if I come home late".

"You want to stay over?" asks Jake.

Daniel hesitates, looking at me.

Jake rolls his eyes "I meant in my room... not hers".

Ally and I laugh.

Daniel smiles, kicks me gently under the table.

"Then yeah, that would be fine".

Jake nods, smiling. “Then why don’t we all go down to High Wycombe?
There’s a film in the cinema we all want to see isn’t there?”

Ally nods. “Yeah okay, let’s go. But Jake, we need to watch out for something”.

Jake frowns, and looks wary. “Watch out for what?”

Ally grins. “We need to make sure that Daniel and Seren do not sit in the back - row”.

We all groan.

(40) Ally.

If my parents saw me riding this fast, they would yell like they have never yelled before, I think suddenly as I ride along. But, at this moment, I don't really care. They can't see me, so it's fine. Besides, if they wanted me to stop riding, why did they never get rid of my bike?

I couldn't help it. It was just there in the garage. I haven't ridden on it for so long. When I saw, I had to get on it, and ride out of the house, just to prove I still could.

I loved bike-riding before I got sick. I used to dream about entering serious competitions. I know that's not possible now. But as I pedal harder, I realise how much I still enjoy it.

It makes me feel alive, reminds me of that fact. The wind hitting my face, dislodging my hat, the burning of my arms and legs, is something I haven't felt since I was thirteen. Three years ago. I couldn't ride on my bike when I was sick. I got tired too easily, so it was too risky.

I got to say, it's times like this, I don't miss having hair. It would just get all messed up and tangled when I rode, mostly because I rode fast. My Mum made me have it long. She wanted to have a little girly girl. I wanted it short. I didn't quite mean bald though....oh well, be careful about what you wish for.

I laugh at my own weird thoughts, and the sensation of wind tickling my scalp. I ignore the aching in my legs, and the tiredness I'm beginning to feel. I pedal faster.

Sometimes I feel a little guilty for enjoying life like this. I wasn't meant to. I was meant to die, not live. Instead, Daniel died.

He was my friend too. And I miss him. Before I got sick, us four, Jake (not too cool to be seen with his little sister), Seren, myself and Daniel would all go down to the woods together. Daniel was hanging out with us, so it must have been after Lily was born. He didn't really socialise before that point. So, we would all go get our bikes, and race each other down to the river, deep in the woods, that we thought only us four knew about. I know now that probably everyone knows about that river. But, no-one else would be there, so to a kids mind…it was our place. It belonged to us.

Jake was the oldest, so automatically he was in charge. Jake is a natural leader, that's hard to deny, but that didn't mean we actually listened to him. Jake eventually would give in, and just have fun himself. But he still had this…watchful eye on us all. Daniel would be kicking around a football, Jake may have joined him, or might have been near Seren, who would be dangling her feet in the river, laughing. And then there would be me, climbing the highest branches of the highest tree. All three would be worrying. We would be chatting and talking, completely casually, but you could tell all three were would slightly nervous about me in the tree. That kind of nervous that makes you laugh and grin.

No-one had to worry. I never fell. I never picked the wrong branch or put my foot on the wrong branch. I just knew where to put my hands and feet, so I could climb up quickly, and ...relatively safely. I hadn't fallen, since I could remember.

It was one of my skills, my childhood. My tendency to be a daredevil.

Until I was 13, and I was thinking about something else. How I felt dizzy and tired, with a headache. I was 13, and I just placed my foot though thin air, and I was dangling by my arms.

I was 13, and of course you think, that you can hang on. Swing your feet back. I had once. But then, your hands get sweaty, and you have to let go.

I fell hard, but I didn't feel any pain for a few moments. I was shocked and surprised. The fact that I had fallen hurt the most. It made me realise what had happened to my body.

Later they all said, "Lucky Jake - a St John cadet was there. Lucky you didn't break any bones. You're so lucky Alexa...." Oh, am I?

But in all honesty, it wasn't been told I had cancer that made me let go of my childhood, it wasn't sitting in that office that made me realise I had to grow up.

It was falling out of that tree.

I probably couldn't climb anything right now. If I tried, I probably would break more than a few bones.

"My body is too damaged", say all the healthcare professionals. I know they are just doing their jobs… but that doesn't make me feel any happier about it.

I think it would be ironic.

I imagine the articles: For the last three years, Alexa Charlotte Smith has battled Acute Myelogenous Leukemia and faced death numerous, tragic times. Tragically, in strange tragic circumstances, she tragically died, after tragically breaking her spine and neck, after tragically climbing a tree, one of her few remaining tragic hobbies, in her incredibly, tragically, short tragic life.

They could at least mention my bike riding.

I laugh out loud, and almost lose control of the bike.

That's when I realise, that I actually have lost control of the bike, am currently going slightly downhill, and potentially about to run over the person that has just come out of one of the houses lining the road.

Oh Crap.

So, I do all I can think to do.

"LOOK OUT".

The person looks around. Oh hell, it's Nathan.

Nathan practically has to dive out of my path.

Luckily, we are on one of those gravel footpaths things, so there are no cars around.

My bike zooms past Nathan, barely missing him. At this point, my bike slows down, and I manage to regain control.

I press the brakes so hard, I think they are about to snap.

Okay, maybe I won't die by climbing trees. Looks like I won't be original after all.

After the noise of the brakes dies away, I hear footsteps behind me.

I turn around to find Nathan, smiling and laughing walking over.

"Had to be you, didn't it Ally?"

I laugh. "I would bow if I wasn't on this bike!"

Nathan rolls his eyes.

"Any reason why you decided to try and run me over?" he says drily.

"It's not like I *tried* to run you over" I point out. "I did warn you".

Nathan laughs. "Yeah, I suppose that's true".

He takes a closer look. “Err…are you okay?”

He’s realised that I’m still on the bike, with no obvious intention of getting off it and is currently slumped over the handlebars.

Instantly his voice becomes tense. “Ally…are you alright?!”

“Pardon? Oh yes, I’m fine…Just….cancer problems….just…give…me a minute.”

Nathan looks …awkward. “Okay…anything I can do?”

“No, no…just hang on”.

I take some breaths and lift my head up.

Nathan seems to instantly relax when I do that.

I brace myself for a second, then lift my leg slowly over the bike. Nathan reaches in to hold the handlebars, keeping the bike still.

With a bit more effect, I manage to get my body off the bike, and my legs onto solid earth without anything falling or collapsing.

“Where are you heading, Ally?” Nathan askes.

I shake my head “I wasn’t. I was just…biking. I used to do it all the time…before I got sick.”

Nathan nods, and looks around. “Where’s your house again? Its up that hill, isn’t it?”

I nod “Back up the hill, and along the road”.

Nathan looks at me. "Maybe, you should head back home?"

"That is a really good idea..."

I reach out for my bike. Nathan shakes his head.

"It's fine. I'll walk it back up for you".

"Nathan, its fine...I can..." I begin to protest.

Nathan gives me a look. My protests literally die.

"its fine, Ally" he insists. "Really".

He turns the bike around, and indicates with his head.

"Shall...we go?"

So, we both start walking.

"So, how come you're down here?" I ask "I thought you lived up in Elm Road?"

Nathan nods "That's right, I do. I was visiting...someone I haven't seen for a while".

"Oh, Callum, you mean?"

Nathan looks at me, a little sharply, so I realise I should explain.

"I live near this road, and I recognised the house you came out of".

"Oh, right!" Nathan looks at me again, hesitates and then asks me something.

"Do...you know Callum then?"

"Callum?" I shake my head "No, not really. But, it's a close neighbourhood, so I know OFF him...and Clarissa".

On hearing her name, Nathan tenses slightly, but then relaxes about a second later.

"...How well did you know her?"

"Less than I know Callum. She seemed...interesting. When I got sick, their mum used to come over, you know, checking how I was, bringing pasta dishes and everything. Clarissa used to come sometimes. We talked a little bit. But I never really knew what to say to her. She was two years older than me, and was just so...selflessly nice".

Nathan smiles "Yeah, she was. She was a little bit of a mystery".

I nod "I never really understood her. She was so different from anyone else".

I wonder whether it's okay to say the next bit, but I think Nathan knows already.

"I knew her enough to know that she loved you" I say quietly.

Nathan looks at me with interest "But you didn't know me back then".

"She talked about you all the time. And when you came to support group and started talking about her...it wasn't hard to work out the rest".

Nathan shakes his head slowly. "I didn't even realise you knew who Clarissa was".

I shrug. "Small world".

He smiles. "Small world. Thank you...for telling me".

I look at him "You already knew she did".

He keeps smiling, and doesn't deny it.

"How long have you known Seren?" he asks a few minutes later. By now, we have slowly made it up the hill, and are coming onto my road.

"Seren? Not to sound cheesy...but I've known her since I can remember. My mum says we went to the same preschool/playgroup thing when we were three? Two maybe? Anyway, that's where we first met apparently. So, that's about thirteen years."

Nathan nods, digests this. "You've always been close?"

I look at him, a little confused about where this is going.

"Yee...sss" I say slowly "we have. We've had our moments, like everyone does, but nothing serious. We've always been best friends"

Nathan murmurs almost to himself. "You would know her better than anyone else".

I think I understand now.

"Jake might disagree with that. Daniel definitely would. But yes, in some ways I would".

Nathan looks at me again. I've never noticed how much his eyes are like Seren's.

"Ally..." he begins.

I interrupt.

"Yes" I say simply.

He frowns. "Yes, to what?" he asks.

By now, we are outside my house. Even though we didn't know this, we've both stopped walking.

"Yes" I say again, but more forcefully. "Yes, I think she does. And yes, I think she would".

Nathan looks confused for a second, then grasps my meaning. He starts smiling. And for a second, the sadness behind his eyes seems to fade.

I take my bike from his unresisting hands.

“Thanks for...walking it up. See you around”.

Nathan shakes his head “It was nothing. Thank you - again”.

I smile “For what?”

He’s still smiling “You already know”.

He lifts his hand in goodbye. Then walks away back down the hill.

His step seems a little lighter.

At that moment, a couple of songs from my favourite band, Mumford and Sons come into my head. There’s Sigh No More, Awake My Soul, After The Storm, and Ghosts That We Knew.

All I can think about is how appropriate the lyrics are.

(41) Seren.

I open the door of my bedroom, really slowly. Then I cautiously look out of my bedroom. I bet I look like one of those Meerkats you see on those wildlife programmes.

Once I judge the coast is clear, I creep out of my bedroom, and down the stairs. It's not like I'm doing anything wrong. It's just that I don't want anyone to see me. But I'm thirsty and I need a drink, so that means leaving my safe zone, and sneaking down for a drink.

Once down the stairs, I make a beeline for the kitchen. On my way, I pass the open - door to the sitting room. Against my better judgement, I glance in the room, as I walk past.

And I see my brother, and my sister lying on the floor, a Monopoly board between them. A game I used to play with Lily, when she didn't want to play Cluedo.

I carry on walking to the kitchen, trying to convince myself it doesn't matter, when I hear what Lily says next.

"Did Seren and Daniel break up?"

I stop walking, almost instantly.

I can't see them, but I can hear Jake's response clearly.

"Why would you think that?"

I lean against the wall, next to the door, and let myself sink, until I'm almost lying on the floor. Their voices float and pierce though the open door. I don't want to see the emotions written on my sister's, and on my brother's face.

I can almost imagine Lily's shrug. "I haven't seen him for AGES...are they on a break?"

Jake sighs. His voice sounds so…different when he finally replies. "Lily, you KNOW what's happened to Daniel."

Lily doesn't miss a beat. "But…but… but…Seren's been….so….grumpy…..and moody - and that happens when grownups break up-from really long-"

Jake interrupts her "Lily. Mum and I told you why Daniel isn't with Seren anymore. And you know they didn't break up."

Lily's silent for ages. That's unusual for her. She usually never stops talking. "Jake…what's death?"

I should go back, to my room, where I can pretend I didn't hear that.

But in a strange way, I want to know what Jake isn't going to say. How he is going to explain death to a six year old girl.

It seems the Monopoly game is abandoned.

"Do you know what life is?" comes Jake's reply.

I can almost her nodding. "Life is when you are alive. It's when you're living".

"Right". Jake replies softly. "So death...is like the opposite of that. It's when life...ends".

Lily considers this "But why does life end?"

"Because that's...life, Lily...It's how you know you lived".

"When does life end?...am I going to die soon!?"

Jake laughs gently, and sadly. "No, Lily. You're not going to die anytime soon. You're not gonna die until you're old and grey".

I think Lily would frown now "Daniel wasn't old and grey".

Jake sighs. Then sighs again. "No, he wasn't".

No, he definitely wasn't.

There's silence again. Lily is always the first to break it.

"Where do you...go when you die?"

I listen to this carefully. If only we knew the answer.

I know Jake will be thinking about how to answer.

"When you die" he says slowly. "You go...wherever you think is right".

Lily seems satisfied with this, and changes the subject.

"Can we play now?"

Jake stays silent for a while, then jerks back into action. “Sure Lily, sure. What piece do you want to be?”

“Ummm....the Car”.

No, she can’t. No. No.

Jake seems surprised. “Not the horse? You’re always the horse”.

“Yeah. But Daniel said I could have HIS piece when he wasn’t playing. I said no, that wouldn’t be fair. But he’s not gonna play ever again, is he? So, the car’s not gonna be used.”

I can hear Jake shifting about, the way he does when he’s nervous or uncomfortable.

Lily changes her mind. “Actually I’ll be the horse... Do you want the car?”

“No, that’s alright. I’ll be the hat”. His usual piece.

I risk a glance into the sitting room.

Lily is now sitting cross-legged, with her head on one side. She’s wearing blue tops and jeans, with her auburn hair curling down her back.

“I know! I’ll give the car to Seren! So, she can remember Daniel!”

Jake stares down, and rearranges the board. “She’s not likely to ever forget him, Lily”.

Lily shrugs. “Just in case she does”.

Jake nods, but doesn't respond. He keeps fiddling with the board. I notice he's placed the little silver dog out. My piece.

Lily picks up the shiny car, and fiddles with it. I want to run over, and just take it off her restless, never still fingers.

"I miss him" she whispers.

Jake looks up slowly. "Daniel?"

I can see her nod, and her fingers keep playing with the car.

"I liked him. He was funny, and nice, and lovely and kind, and nice, and sporty… and…." Lily breaks off into a sob.

Jake moves into a cross-legged position, and reaches across the board to stroke his sister's hair.
"Hey now, he liked you too".

"No he didn't!"

Jake shuffles himself, so he's sitting next to her, and both are facing away from me. He has his arm around her back.

"Yeah, he did! He thought you were sweet, and funny, and...just adorable".

Lily sniffs. "He said I was annoying!"

Jake laughs. "When did he say that?"

"Two years ago!"

Jake gently nudges her. "Well, you were four then..."

"So?"

"You *were* an annoying little girl".

She was pretty annoying. She was always following everyone about, with puppy dog eyes asking for food and attention and toys. Daniel was good with her. She was so small. When she latched on to my foot, Daniel picked her up, and threw up and down in his arms, making her giggle, whilst yelling dramatically "You're annoying!" He did love Lily through.

Lily pushes Jake hard. "That's mean!"

Jake pretends to fall on the ground. He's laughing.

Lily starts to giggle.

Jake sits up. "Do you remember that time where he and Seren had an argument, and she came back here, completely frustrated?"

Lily nods eagerly "Yeah, yeah! And Daniel followed her home, and sat her outside her bedroom door, until she let him in. And then....I saw them KISSING!"

"Yeah, I saw *that".* Jake says drily. "I think we both saw too much of *that".*

I want to smile, but I've forgotten how.

So Lily smiles and laughs for me.

"Jake....?" she asks.

"Yeah, Lily?"

She takes a deep breath "Did Daniel love Seren?"

Jake smiles sadly, but his eyes still shine with happiness behind them. "Yes, he did. Very much. He loved her a lot."

I'm forgetting a lot of things today. First I can't smile. Now I can't breathe.

Lily looks up at Jake. Her blue eyes do that old puppy dog thing. But they seem wider, more desperate this time."

"Does Seren still love Daniel?" she asks.

Jake inhales deeply, and exhales. "Yes, she does".

So, I haven't forgotten how to cry. That's always good.

"Does Seren still love me?" She blurts out in a rush. "Not like she...loves Daniel, but does she still....like me?"

I want to breathe and scream. I want to yell. Just shut up, Lily, just shut up! You don't know what you're talking about.

Jake leans forward, on to his knees. Lily immediately mirrors his position.

Jake places both his hands on her shoulders, and looks deep into her eyes.

"Listen Lily" he begins.

And you can shut up too, Jake! Please, be quiet. None of you know anything! You never did. You don't understand either!

"Seren loves you very much".

I try to yell, to scream, but just an empty puff of air comes. I'm mute, and I can taste the salty tears.

I can hear Jake still talking.

"You're her only sister. And Daniel loved you too. Believe me, she doesn't hate you, she never did".

Lily struggles to find words "But why...?"

"Has she been acting like this?" Jake finishes. "Because...she doesn't know what else to do. She's lost, and confused, and angry".

"Angry at me?" she asks, her eyes open wide.

"No" Jake says firmly "Not at you. Believe me, if she hated you, she wouldn't be acting like this with you at all".

He takes his hands off her shoulders.

He looks down at her hands, still clutching the car.

"Why don't you keep the car, Lily?"

Lily looks down at it surprised, as if she didn't think she was holding it.

She looks back up at our brother. "But…what about Seren…or you?"

Jake smiles "We've got plenty to remember him by. You, though…don't have as much".

Lily still looks unsure.

Jake rolls his eyes gently "Lily, Dan would want you to have it." He would, He really would have.

Anyway, it seals it for Lily. Her confused face breaks out into a wide smile.

She practically throws herself at Jake, into a hug which knocks him down to the floor.

She then runs upstairs to put the car in her treasure box.

Jake laughs gently.

There's no noise for a while.

"I know what I said was true, Seren" he calls out. "I wasn't just making it up, to make her feel better".

I jump up, startled, and make a runner for the stairs.

Jake doesn't follow me, but carries on calling out. "You're NOT the bitch you're pretending to be!"

And I want to believe it. But maybe, I would have. But what else could I be?

I don't know if I'm pretending.

Nothing makes sense, nothing at all.

Not even Nathan.

(42) Daniel.

What do we say to the God of death?

Not today.

This proves to my parents that watching Game of Thrones is actually good for you, as it teaches you philosophical ideas.

Sometimes there isn't a tomorrow. And sometimes you don't get the chance to say anything to Death - I wouldn't say it was a God. It's just inevitable.

I feel like I'm suffocating. Suffocating in the 'thin white sheet'. But also floating. Floating in memories.

If you try to swim, you become tired. But you can float for ages. Preserve what energy you have left.

I don't know how long I have. Probably not that long.

But the memories don't hurt as much anymore.

I can't remember the first time I actually saw Seren. Our parents had been friends for so long, it seems like I've always known her.

But I do know the time where I actually looked at her, and really saw her.

Her little sister had just been born.

My mum dragged me over there. Because Dad wasn't there, and she couldn't leave me alone.

I sat on the sofa, whilst my mum, chatted softly with Seren's mum, about how sweet the new baby was.

When the front door opened.

Jake came in first. He gave me a nod. He didn't know me that well. I didn't actually socialise.

Then, close behind him, came Seren.

And I smiled at her. Because I saw her.

I still don't know what it was. What I saw.

But it was like, I saw who she was. What she was. What she is.

Incredible.

That's the only word I can use to describe about how I saw her that day.

There's no words to describe what and who Seren Ambern is.

There's words that can be used to describe her. But there's no word to describe who a person is, when all those words are combined into one.

So I have to improvise. The word I use is:

Seren.

Just as I begin to feel slightly awkward about standing outside a theatre alone, she comes off the bus looking confused, and lost. She turns around, but because off the crowds she can't see me. She turns again, looking slightly panicked.

I lift up my hand and wave. Thankfully she sees. The lost panicked look is gone, instantly replaced with a smile. She waves back, and begins to weave through the crowds, gathering outside the theatre.

She finally makes it to me. Her auburn hair, wild and loose. A spark in her intelligent eyes. A red flush around her cheeks. She looks breathless, and happy.

She laughs lightly. "Hi, thought you had stood me up!"

I laugh back. "I was worried you weren't going to turn up!"

"Are you kidding?! I've wanted to see this for ages!"

We both laugh again. Then don't say anything. Just smile at each other.

Seren drops her eyes, smiling. A tiny giggle escapes.

I indicate the door. "Um...shall we go in?"

She raises her eyes. "Um yes! We should".

We don't move for a few seconds.

Nervously, I offer her my hand. Slowly, she takes it.

We laugh again.

And together we walk into the theatre.

"You know-I'm glad you didn't pick something overly romantic". She comments, just before the performance starts.

I look at her, curiously. "How come?"

She shrugs. "Well, There're kind of cliché aren't they? I mean, girl in love with boy. Bit of comedy thrown in...not much of a storyline really".

I look at her and start laughing.

She looks confused, but not offended or anything.

"What's so funny?" She asks, sounding amused.

"Oh...nothing...it's just..."

She laughs "Go on! Tell me! I won't be offended!"

I breathe in, to stop laughing.

"Because I'm with the only girl I have ever met that will never force her boyfriend to go watch a romantic film with her".

She looks at me, with raised eyebrows, and a secret grin, looking like she's got some kind of incredible idea.

"Is that what you are, then? My boyfriend...?

I stumble over my words, laughing all the time "Well…um, in the future….after all…"

Seren grins and watches me with laughter filling her face, and a look I have never seen before.

Before I can answer, a loud BOOM sounds.

And the play has started.

With last smiles at each other, we turn our attention to the stage.

"Does this feel sort of weird to you?" she asks later, as we walk home together.

I look at her, studying her face "What does?"

She shrugs "All of this….I mean….people always say it should feel awkward….and we've known each other for a while….but it doesn't. It feels…. I don't know…"

I raise my eyebrows "You don't know, huh? That's a first!"
She glares playfully, "Oh shut up!"

I laugh "Not a chance".

She rolls her eyes "And there's the Daniel I know!"

I stop walking for a second. Seren stops as well, looking at me.

"No..." I say slowly "It doesn't feel awkward....does it? It feels....right".

Seren smiles, and I know I've echoed her thoughts exactly.

I take her hand, and we carry on walking....well, it's not quite walking, but there's no other word for it.

"Seren. It's quite an interesting name". I say thoughtfully, stirring hot chocolate.

Seren sits across, sipping her own drink. "Is it?"

It's been a week since the Tempest, and we're meeting in Starbucks after school, even though we don't actually like Coffee. But I learnt quickly that Seren's favourite hot drink is hot chocolate, and Starbucks do the best, with marshmallows and whipped cream.

We also found out that they do the best strawberry cheesecake (Seren's favourite) and the best hot triple chocolate giant brownies (my favourite).

I nod. "Well, yeah. I've never heard someone with that name."

Seren smiles. "You've never been to Wales then?"

"No....'fraid not. It's a common name over there then?"
She nods slowly "Well...I think so. I haven't been over there for a while....but it is a Welsh name."

I sip my coffee "Does it mean anything?"

Seren blushes "Yeee...sss......but it's totally embarrassing!"

I nudge her gently "Oh come on, we've known each other since we were little kids. I know nearly every embarrassing thing about you!"

She slowly shakes her head "The problems with going out with a boy who's known you for ages!"

"C'mon....tell me....I'll buy you another drink."
She laughs "Oh...fine...I can't resist hot chocolate!"

"So, what does it mean?"

She sighs dramatically, and meets my eyes. "Star".

"Come again?"

She gives me a pointed look. "It means star".

"How is that embarrassing?!"

She looks defensive. "Well...think about it. It's just...it's patronising....and".

"I think it's cute".

She points at me. "See! Right there! Reason it's embarrassing".

I laugh. "Well... it's actually kind of appropriate".

"How so...?"

"Ah. Well, *star*....I've always wanted to see a meteorite ...but I'll settle for you".

She looks at me, looking confused, amused and still defensive
"And...why?"
"Because a shooting star is a meteorite....which is a ball of fire, and you can get 'shooting' angry and then get fiery".

I grin at her, feeling very pleased with myself...until I see Seren's face.

"Daniel" she says cool, calm and collected. "Let me explain something to you..."

I only have time to say "bloody hell!", before I'm pulled into a science lesson, I didn't know I was getting.

"JUST GO AWAY!" she yells as she storms up her driveway, to get into her home, to get away from me.

We've been together for a while now and I've lost count of how many times we've been out together, how many debates we've had, how many good times we've had.

But I haven't lost count of how many fights we've had. One - starting today.

"OH COME ON!" I yell back. "I DIDN'T MEAN IT!"

She scoffs.

"YES, YOU BLOODY DID!"

I pause.

"OKAY...I MIGHT HAVE DONE... but I didn't mean it about you!"

She laughs "Yeah right!"

She fumbles with her keys.

Her auburn hair is wild and flustered. Her blue eyes bright, with tears she won't show, and pure anger.

And she looks beautiful.

She finally manages to open the door, and I get a brief glance of Jake, looking extremely amused and but slightly confused. I also get a brief look at Lily who yells out:

"That's why I'm never having a boyfriend!"

Jake raises an eyebrow at me, and the door slams shut.

I breathe out hard. This whole thing is stupid.

But it was kind of my fault.

I didn't realise she would get upset though.

So, I fidget slightly, and then walk up to knock on the door.

Jake opens it, just before Seren yells out: "Jake, if you dare let him in, I swear...."

Jake puts his head to one side and calls out.

"You swear what?"

"Jake!" I hear her yell out again.

"Seren!" he mimics.

Seren then lets loose with some language I didn't even knew, that she knew.

Jake really looks like he's going to laugh.

"Very nice, sis." he says dryly. He sighs dramatically. "Listen, if you're going to have arguments with Daniel.... try not to bring it home. Life here is hard enough!"

I can just about hear Seren's muffled response. Judging by the giggles, Lily did too.

Jake looks at me, and raises an eyebrow at me.

"Wow. You sure you can take her?"

"Actually...it was sort of my fault."

Jake laughs out loud

"*Sort of* your fault?"

I shift uncomfortably.

"Well...I didn't realise she would react like *that*".

Jake rolls his eyes.

"You've known her since we were all little kids, and you didn't realise something about her?"

I nod reluctantly, which makes Jake laugh again.

"Well…now you do!"

"All I said was that…." I start.

Jake cuts me off.

"I don't need to know…just sort it out. One of my sisters is already a nightmare…. No Lily, I am definitely NOT talking about you…I don't need two of them acting like demons".

He steps away from the door, to let me in.

"You know where her room is - she's probably beginning to calm down now".

I climb up the stars, whilst Jake remains downstairs, trying to explain to Lily something about 'teenage moods'.

Seren's white door is firmly shut.

I knock on it. "Seren?"
"Daniel?" I hear her say quietly "Please just go away".

"Hey…just hear me out. I'll just talk though the door…you don't have to listen".

I don't hear a 'no', so I start talking.

"I'm sorry I said what I said. It a stupid thing I heard from a mate of mine. At the time, I thought it was hilarious. And like any male our age, I didn't think about what it could mean to someone. But I don't believe it...I thought it was stupid, that's why I thought it was funny. I should have thought about it, a bit more."
I lean against the door and sigh.

Seren replies in a tiny voice. "Yep...you should have...But I shouldn't have reacted the way I did. And I'm sorry..."

"No...No" I cut off. "You've got nothing to be sorry for..."

I hear her take a deep breath. "Yes I do...you must think I'm a complete idiot".

I deny this instantly "Of course I don't. I think it's great that you're so passionate. You're not scared to voice your opinions, your feelings, and your thoughts."

I smile inwardly. "And it's one of the many reasons I love you" I think, until I realised that I've spoken out loud.

"What?" I hear Seren say.

I burn with embarrassment, but shake it off

"I love you" I state.

I hear Seren's almost inaudible gasp, and a tiny laugh.

"I love you too".

I smile in disbelief.

"Seriously?"

She doesn't answer, but she opens the door.

I walk in slowly. She stands by the window, and the evening light shines on her.

"Daniel"

"Seren",

In a couple of steps, I stride over to her, and just wrap her in my arms, firmly. It's like she fits perfectly. Like I was made for holding her.

She wraps herself around me. I never knew what it would feel like. That it would feel so...indescribable.

She laughs once, in happiness, in wonder.

And before I realise it, we're kissing. And laughing.

And full of wonder.

I don't know how long we were like this. But every second, seemed like minutes. And we couldn't get enough.

It was like, we had to make this moment count. Who could tell if we would have another? What if we didn't?

Then we heard a tiny gasp.

We sprang apart...to find little Lily standing in the open doorway, her eyes wide open.

And Jake walking up behind her.

He takes one glance, at the looks on both our faces, rolls his eyes. Then, steers Lily away, with his hands on both her shoulders.

Not before shutting the door.

(43) Seren.

I walk over to the treadmill, and am about to get on it. When the doorbell goes.

I sigh more dramatically than I need to be. As Jake's in the shower, and Lily's not actually here, I head over to the door.

And open to reveal…Nathan.

He looks up, a strange look in his eyes when he sees me.

We look at each other slightly awkwardly, and he dips his head.

"Hello" he says quietly, a small smile lightening up his face.

"Hi" I say back.

He nods towards the hallway. "Uh…can I come in?"
"Oh! Um…sure".

I step away, to let him in.

He steps forward, and I shut the door.

He looks around "Is Jake…around? He asked me to come over."

I smile, despite myself.f "Calculus again?"

He gives a small laugh "Not quite…*he's* helping me with Geography".

I laugh as well "He's in the shower…he should be out in a minute. Um….do you want a drink?"

He looks slightly awkward "Um...well, if it's not too much trouble".

I shrug "Course not...Come on through".

I lead him through to the Kitchen, where he takes a seat.

To my relief, I have to turn my back to him, as I get some glasses out. It helps take away some of the guilt.

"So...what do you want to drink then?" I say, busily.

"Um...water's fine".

I nod and fill up a glass. I place it down in front of Nathan.

I begin to turn away again, when he slightly places his hand over mine.

Startled, I look up at him. The look in his eyes is so familiar but so different.

"Seren." He says slowly and gently.

I'm already shaking my head "No...please don't".

He continues to look at me "Seren...just deny it. Just deny that you don't feel it. I know I can't".

I don't try to pull free...but I can't do this.

"You don't understand" I whisper.

He gently places his other hand over my own.

"Seren, you deserve to be happy" he whispers. "You can't live for Daniel's ghost".

And it's the word 'deserve' that gets me.

"But I don't!" I scream at him. "How can I deserve to be happy!?"

I pull my hand free, and I feel alone and cold again. I feel nothing but numbness and guilt.

"How can I be happy when he's dead?!" I yell "I KILLED him! I can't be happy! I don't deserve to be!"

Nathan stands up, and knows enough, not to come any nearer. He extends his arm in a calming gesture.

I'm too far gone.

"You didn't kill Clarissa!" I carry on. "You're completely innocent! You're free to move on with your life! You can! But I'm a murderer okay?! I ended a life. And I scared! I'm scared that feeling anything, will make me forget what I am. If I feel anything, I'll start to move on. I'll forget him! And I loved him! I'll forget the guilt...And when he came back...it was alright at first. I hadn't completely lost him! But he's gone again! He's not coming back! I've caused him to leave twice!"

I didn't mean to say all that to Nathan. But it's gone on to far now. It all has.

I realise I'm shrieking. And Jake, finally out of the shower, is standing in the doorway.

I don't know how long he's been there, but I don't care.

It's gone on too far.

I push past Nathan. He tries to stop me.

But I grab the glass of water and throw the water in his face.

He has to let me go.

Jake tries to restrain me.

But I elbow him away, and I'm out of the kitchen.

I head to the treadmill, but realise it's not enough.

And before I know it, I'm running out of the front door, onto the street.

I'm not coming back.

(44) Clarissa.

If I was still alive, right now I would be taking in deep breaths. But I don't actually breathe anymore....

No...No...No.

I could try and be philosophical, and say that what I just saw was happening for a reason. But that's not going to help anyone.

And it's not going to help Nathan or Seren.

Seren needs Nathan, even though she can't admit it. Nathan can erase the guilt in her. He can bring back from the brink, bring her back to life.

Nathan needs Seren. He needs to forget me.

Because, after all, what am I?
Well...I don't know. But I think I'm just memories. Fragments of life that never left.

Nathan's almost there. He's almost let go. Seren can help him. If he can stop her from burning herself out.

But it's almost too late.

I can see what's happening, and what will happen.

I was idiotic, I was stupid.

Nathan's scared of doing what we must do. Or rather, what they must do.

I still hang over him. His memories of me are still there.

And he never knew where I was, what happened to me, whether I had forgiven him?

Do I blame him for what happened to me?

Of course I don't. I never forgave, because they were nothing to forgive.

It all seems that we become blind to those we love.

We say and mean something. But sometimes, it doesn't apply to those they love.

Oh, humanity.

How I miss it.

Why did I stay?

It all comes clear. They all say things become clear at the end.

But it's not quite the end. Not yet. But it soon will be. For me. And for Seren, if Nathan doesn't get there in time.

Why did I stay?

I was so busy musing on everything else, I failed to notice myself.

But I now know. I've always known. It was woven in everything the fragments that were left of me did.

Watched.

I miss life. But I miss one person in particular.

I know who.

I couldn't let go either.

And I have to fix this.

Until this moment, I watched, but I didn't interfere - except in one moment.

But I now realise, that just the memories of me interfered with Nathan.

And I may not be anything anymore. But I still have a conscience. I still have morals.

I have to help. I have to interfere. For Nathan. To make it right by him.

I loved philosophy when I was alive.

And now everything I thought, everything I decided, tumbles around my thoughts.

A house is not a home. A home is not a house.

Home is love. Home is those you love. Home is the people you chose to be with.

And now I make a decision. A temporary one.

I'm going home.

I thought it was impossible. But now I realise how easy it is.

Let yourself float. Let yourself fall.

Let yourself forget about gravity.

Remember home.

Let memories guide you there.

(45) Daniel.

I knew she would do something stupid. It's her passion, but also her guilt.

I want to help. I need to help. I'm fighting, and kicking. But it won't give.

Seren. SEREN. I'm yelling. Just hoping she will hear me.

Still kicking. I'm been fighting since I came back, since she broke the frequency.

Somehow, I still tired. How is that possible? I'm not human anymore.

Or maybe, I still am.

But it doesn't matter. It's Seren. I'll always have energy to save her.

When I was alive, all I wanted to do is protect her. Help her. Support her.

But what I only just begin to realise, but what I already knew, is that the most difficult thing is to save someone from their self.

But for now, I have to be like Seren. Achieve the impossible.

And I can do that. For her.

The thin white sheet, still refuses to break, even tear.

I'll keep kicking, punching it, and doing what I need to do.

I want her to be happy. If Nathan can make her happy, then I'll personally take her to him.

But she needs to let go of her guilt.

And I need to get to her. Because she is doing something incredibly stupid. And I need to stop her. Before it is too late.

And it can't be. It's not time

Seren has fate. She has time. She has destiny.

She's going to live until she's 95 - maybe 100.

She's going to have children, nieces, nephews, grandchildren, great grandchildren.

She's going to go to medical school. She's going to be the best doctor ever. She's not going to give in.

She wants to go to UCL, but she can make it to Cambridge.

She'll help Ally.

She'll find a cure for cancer.

She'll love Nathan.

She'll marry him, in a whirlwind ceremony.

She'll join Mensa.

She'll laugh again.

She'll get on with Lily again.

She'll be happy.

She'll be incredible. She already is.

And all this can't go.

I won't let it.

SEREN. I kick, and fight harder, than I ever have before.

Harder and harder.

And, like some miracle, I see a tear.

I'm no longer trapped.

I can get though.

I don't need encouragement.

I'm through.

(46) Nathan.

Her long hair streams lose behind her. She forgot to re-tie it, before we went. Luckily, there isn't much wind tonight, so it remains tangle-free, and streaming gold.

After a quick explanation to her mum, about where we were going, which didn't take long as I thought, we immediately got our bikes, and started biking down towards the National Trust park that is nearby her house.

"My parents trust me" she says, over the sound of our bikes on gravel. "And they know what I'm like with my strange obsessions".

I laugh. "It's hardly strange, Rissa".

She laughs back. "Everything about humanity is strange".

"You've got that right, love".

She looks at me with surprise, and also happiness, and I realise that's the first time I have said that to her.

But there's no time to say anything else because we've arrived at the gate that will lead into the park. We need to walk up a hill, to get to the best spot.

By mutual agreement, we leave our bikes by the gate, and walk up the hill, with our hands entwined.

It's the middle of summer, so even though it's the middle of the night, we don't feel cold wearing only t - shirts and jeans.

The hill is quite high but not steep, so it's doesn't take us to long to reach the top.

I wish the walk had taken a little longer.

Clarissa lets go of my hand, and gazes up. One of the things I love so much about her is the look of wonder and peaceful serenity she gets, every time she sees the stars.

And when we are both lying down, on the cool dry, grass, I can see why. Up here, we are far away from light pollution. We can see stars from miles away, all shining bright.

It's hard to comprehend at this moment that all stars are simply ball of gases, burning hundreds of miles away in space.

"You know we are looking back in time, when we look up at the stars" I say aloud. "What we're looking at may have already come and gone".

"Yes, I know that" murmurs Clarissa from next to me. "But maybe, just maybe, time is irrelevant. Maybe time is just a concept that humanity invented to help us comprehend the true miracles of the world".

She turns her head towards me, tearing her gaze from her stars. "Imagine that time was just a word, people used to use to try and understand things, thinking that everything in the world could be explained."

"When sometimes nothing can". I say, echoing her thoughts. She rubs off on me, in more ways than any of us will know.

The stars shine down on us, illuminating her gentle face. No, somethings can never be explained.

Then I have another thought. "Up there, some stars are exploding into supernovas, forming elements, heavier than iron. And then...they are ejected into the universe".

Clarissa continues to gaze up at the stars. "To form new planets and new stars".

"And then some life may form, though God knows how".

"It doesn't matter how it forms though. What matters is that life may start."

"Then that life will eventually end. Our elements will return to the universe".

I can almost see Clarissa smile next to me. But I don't look. I'm watching the stars.

"And then our elements will make new stars and planets" she whispers softly. "It never ends, love... We never truly go. What made us, who we are, floats around the world and universe, forming new life, in many new forms. Some of the stars we are looking at now, may be forming elements that will, in their future, form you and me".

We don't say anything for a while. It's a comfortable silence. It's just that you can't say much to that.

"That's the North Star" I finally say, pointing. "The brightest star in the night sky".

"Sailors used to use stars to guide themselves home, you know. They only had to look up for that star, and they would know which way was North". Rissa replies.

I notice another star directly above, where I know Clarissa is lying on the grass.

"Do you know that star, Rissa?"

She looks. "No…but do you?"

I smile, knowing she can't see. "I do now. It's your star".

I don't know which one of us got up first, or who started humming first.

But the two of us danced, in the middle of the night, under the stars that exploded and watched, under the moon that showed us where to step, on the cool grass that tickled and moved under her bare feet.

As Rissa twirled in my arms, her gold hair spinning, her emerald eyes laughing, I made a promise to myself.

I would come clean. I didn't know how to, or how long it would take. But for Rissa, I would. I would let her be the only drug I needed.

I would also remember this moment for all my life, so I could honour the girl I loved with my memories.

I would find a way to make the girl I loved as happy as I was at this moment.

It took me awhile, but I like to believe I achieved all three of those things.

And now, I need to keep achieving them.

It's late. She's been gone for hours. Her and Jake's mum has already called the Police. A women, who I realise is Daniel's mother, sits at the kitchen table with her.

Jake and I are in the sitting room. We're not allowed to help in the search.

Jake paces, and mutters to himself. It doesn't take a genius to work out what he's thinking.

I'm blaming myself as well. And this time, it is my fault. Jake claims it isn't. Turns out he saw the whole thing.

And he's not an idiot. He knew.

Oh god. Seren…

She needs help. She's stuck in her own head, in her own guilt.

I should have helped more.

I saw the signs. I did the same when Clarissa died.

I said what she needed to know.

I thought I had helped.

She was opening up.

What happened?

I bury my face in my hands.

She's gone running.

She's running away.

And I understand. She's running away from me.

We've told the police what she said. We were the last ones to see her, after all.

And now, they're looking for a hysterical, potentially suicidal, young teenager.

I shouldn't have said anything.

But she needs help.

I send up a silent prayer, up to anyone who's listening. If Daniel really is still here, if some part of Clarissa, is still here, I hope they're listening.

I swear, if you bring Seren back ...safe, I'll stay away from her, if that's what she wants. I'll stay away...I won't forget Clarissa. I won't burn with her. But please, help her. Find a way to help her. She needs it. I'll be whatever she wants, a friend, and an enemy. I'll be what you want. Just bring her home.

Jake's left the room. He's gone into the bathroom. He doesn't like people seeing him lose his composure. Judging by the sounds of running water, and splashes, he's going to be in there for a while.

I look up at the sky. No stars.

How appropriate.

I carry on looking, in some kind of hope. If a star appears, it could be someone listening to my silent promise. I'll know she'll have heard it.

It'll be some kind of sign of hope. That she'll come back.

That the meteorite won't burn out.

And by some miracle, a cloud shifts, revealing...the brightest star I have ever seen. The brightest star I never thought to see again.

And I don't know what makes me suddenly move onto my feet.

But that star means more than I hoped. It's telling me more than I hoped.

Clarissa.

Seren. SEREN.

I know where she is.

I don't even think. I just run.

Someone yells.

I yell back.

I don't hear her reply.

But I don't care.

Right now, I only care about one thing.

It's not too late.

I glance up. The star still shines. It follows me.

I carry on running.

I run across the street, and up the road.

And I almost miss it, in the dark.

But I find the gate that leads into the woods

Without hesitation, I go though.

It had to be here.

Here, I saw the Star - Clarissa's star, for the first time.

The star that brought me back from the edge.

Tonight, I, myself will bring another person back from the edge.

I couldn't save Clarissa. But I can save Seren.

I yell her name, more than once. I lose count of many times I yell and scream it out.

And for one moment, I could have sworn, that I heard two other voices yelling with me. And one I recognise.

(47) Seren.

I don't know where I am. I don't care.

It needs to end. There's a reason I feel guilt.

A reason he came back.

We need to swap places.

My mind unravels, and winds again.

Strange thoughts emerge.

Someone had to die. It wasn't Ally.

And it wasn't Daniel.

It should have been me.

I can put it right.

I can change everything.

I'll go. I'll leave.

It'll bring him back.

My mind still retains some of its rationality, but it's more of an under - thought than anything.

If I go, I'll be with him. If he can't come back, I'll go to him. We're meant to be together. We only make sense together. In life and death.

He came back for that small time. To tell me that. To get me to follow him.

But I messed it up.

I met Nathan.

I let him, Ally and Jake push me towards moving on. In other words, forgetting him.

Why did I listen?
How stupid was I?

But at the end, all things become clear.

I understand now.

I understand two different conflicting thoughts. But they all slide together.

It doesn't matter which one is true.

All that matters, is that I'm putting it all right.

And I'll see Daniel, very soon, in one way or another.

I carry on running. I can taste pure adrenaline, pure mindlessness, and pure wildness. It echoes with a finality.

I laugh. It echoes through the woods I now recognise.

I'm breathing hard, with exhilaration and excitement.

The ground feels muddy and swampy beneath my feet.

I'm running next to a strong river.

The rains have made it torrential, and it rushes past me, in a sound that echoes the noise in my ears, and fits with the thundering I hear.

I carry on running, next to the river. When I slip. When I fall.

For a moment, everything seems slow. Then I'm in the water which bangs against me harder than anything.

I don't try to swim. As each wave hits me, I see memories.

Memories of Daniel.

It's over. I'm ending it.

I don't swim. My body feels too heavy. I wouldn't swim anyway.

I close my eyes. And let the water, take me where it wants.

Let it wash away my guilt, all my emotions. Let it let me go. Let me leave life. And go to the next chapter.

(48) Nathan.

I stop for a second. I heard a noise I recognised.

"SEREN!"

No answer.

In some kind of hope, I glance up at Clarissa's star. It's moved away

It's a stupid superstition. But it's Clarissa.

I run towards it.

And I see the river.

And I realise.

Oh.....God....no.

I run to the riverbank.

Oh...please...

It's not too late. It can't be.

I look at the way that the current is flowing.

And I look down it, mentally following the current.

And I see her.

"SEREN!"

Following instincts, without thinking, I'm in the water.

I choke. I tread water.

The current pushes me, trying to take me with it,

But no, not today.

For one second, I look up. The star shines bright. I know she's helping. I also know the boy that loved her first will not let her die tonight.

I swim against it.

Desperation makes me stronger.

Every stroke hurts. Every paddle I make is draining.

But I'm not giving in.

Not in a million years.

I saved her once. When I first met her.

I can save her again.

The water's cold and stings.

Seren's been in it longer than I have.

Seren.

With a few more strokes, I propel myself forward.

And I've got her.

"Seren! Seren?! Oh, crap, Seren!"

If Daniel and Clarissa are here tonight. I need them now. We're in the middle of the river. If we are going to live, we need to get back to the river bank.

But I can't let go of Seren.

Will Daniel let her die? Will Clarissa let me die?

I know the answers to both those questions.

I was scared, that I would be hurt again. That if I let someone back into my life, they would leave.

But now, I trust completely.

I let the water take us.

And a different current bangs against us. Pushing us away from the middle of the river.

And on to the riverbank.

Where I can pull us both onto firmer ground.

I breathe for a second. Then turn to unconscious Seren.

I started St John Ambulance, after Rissa died. I wanted to be able to save people, even though I couldn't save Clarissa.

I never thought I would have to.

I shake her gently.

I check her airway.

DR ABC.

Danger. For the First Aider. Even if there was, I wouldn't leave.

Response: No response.

Airway: Airway clear.

Breathing: I listen. I look for the rising and falling of her chest.

Circulation: Colour comes back slowly when I pinch her finger.

I've still got time.

I pull her top off.

It doesn't matter about modesty. I'm saving her life.

Begin CPR.

Thirty chest compressions. To the tune of Staying Alive.

I tilt her head back. My hands become sticky with blood. She must have hit her head.

Pinch her nostrils. Breathe two breaths down her throat.

I know the drills. But they don't help me,

Come on, Seren, come on.

(49) Seren.

Everything's white. I blink in wonder. Did it work? Where am I? I'm not Christian, so I don't think Heaven applies to me. It won't apply to me, even if I was.

So why is everything so white?

Is it meant to be peaceful? Meant to be pure?

But it just seems unnatural. It's to white, to bright, to be right.

But how can it not be right?

I did the right thing for once.

But if I am dead, more things don't feel right. I shut my eyes. I can feel something pulling me back down to Earth. I'm not free.

Something stops me from taking another step. And I understand. Behind me, is my earth - self. In front of me, is death.

I'm at a crossroads.

It seems a slim hope, but I know he'll be waiting "Daniel?"

He appears instantly, taking my breath away.

My memories no longer do him justice. He looks stronger, healthier. His eyes gleam more than I remember, his hair shines more.

But he also blends in. Something about him, is part of the white that surrounds us.

You're not human.

He smiles, and nods like he heard my thought.

No, I'm something else.

He steps forward. "Seren".

I close my eyes. I missed his voice.

When I open them, he's holding both my hands.

"I should have realised you would do something stupid" he says, shaking his head, but his eyes still smile.

"It wasn't stupid" I whisper.

Daniel smiles. Was it his smile I first loved?

"It was *incredibly* stupid, Seren. I think you can see that. Because even though you do stupid things, you are not."

I know he's speaking the truth. I know that he knows, that I know.

But that doesn't mean that I going to actually admit it.

"It's my fault. It always been my fault. You died for me...it should have been me...not you."

Daniel shakes his head firmly. "No. No Seren. It was never you. It was always me".

He looks me in the eyes. "The universe has plans for you".

I deny this instantly "Only because you died! It would have been you that the universe planned for".

He laughs gently "God, you're so stubborn!" He lets go of my hand, and rests his hand on my cheek. "Listen, you've almost died three times, right? - the car with me, the car with Nathan...and now".

I frown, thinking about this. Sighing, I nod.

He continues. "And you've been saved three times. Once by me, and twice by Nathan....face it ....it's not your time to die".

I struggle to comprehend this. But, as much as I hate to admit it...I think, he's right.

"But...I..." I can't speak. All I can say. "It's not rational".

Daniel smiles. "The world never is".

I realise I'm crying now.

"C'mon Seren. You know I'm right" he continues. "And Nathan's waiting for you".

He thinks for a moment, then smiles "Actually, I think Nathan has saved you more times than you know."

"I think I love him" I say honestly and still crying.

Daniel smiles "Good. He loves you".

I have to squint now to actually see him now. He's fading in now. It's almost over, this strange moment.

He notices this as well. His face, takes on a look of acceptance.

He looks at me seriously. "Seren...let go of me. Let go of the guilt. I would have died anyway. Maybe not that day. Maybe not the day after. But one day soon. Just let go. Let yourself love Nathan".

"But" I whisper. "If I love Nathan, I'll forget you. I won't love you anymore".

He looks at me tenderly. "Oh Seren...some things you have to forget. Sometimes you have to forget, so you can move on. But the amazing thing about moving on is...you keep the important memories. And you'll always love me. But in a different way to how you will love Nathan. You're going to go to med school. You're going to have the best life possible. And I'll see you again. One day. In a different life, in a different time..."

And ever since Daniel died, I fully accept what he's saying. He studies the expressions on my face. And he looks happy when he realises that I've accepted it.

And then I realise, and I accept it. "I'm not going to see you again am I? At least...not in this lifetime".

Daniel shakes his head. "No...I can leave now. You're going to be happy. I can enter the doorway now. I can enter the next chapter".

He smiles at me and kisses me on my forehead. "Go home now" He begins to walk away, the whiteness begins to swallow him.

But there's one more final thing.

"Daniel" I call.

He turns around, but carries on walking "Yeah?"

"When you were dying, you whispered something to me...what was it?"

I hear him laugh, even though I can't see him anymore. "What do you think?"

I smile as I realise. "Daniel....I love you too.

And that's when I start to fall back to Earth. And I can see the stars, shining, shining bright.

Like every person, instead of accepting a painful truth, we run. Because we still have that hope that the painful truth isn't a truth.

But, eventually, you have to push down your fears, and turn around.

And face the truth.

And it hurts. But it brings peace and salvation.

And I'm not afraid anymore. I embrace it. I accept it.

I'm alive.

(50) Daniel.

I keep walking, letting the white swallow me. It brings peace. And now, I'm finally saying goodbye. Seren's finally forgiven herself. She's going to be happy. And I'm leaving. And I don't know where. But that's okay. I'll be absorbed into the white. My atoms will come loose and free. And who knows? Maybe there'll form another person, another male, in another life time.

I laugh. And shut my eyes. I've had my time now. And time eventually runs out.

But it carries on in others.

I'm entering the unknown. I fear nothing. I'm simply entering another chapter, another story. Another life. Just a doorway.

No point complaining. I would have loved to grow old with Seren, but...I couldn't. And someone else will. And that person is the luckiest in the world.

I breathe out deeply, letting the last bit of my soul, leave my non-existent form. I smile. And I'm gone.

(51) Nathan.

Seren coughs back at me. She finally breaths.

"Seren?" She's still unconscious though. I gently swipe away some of her damp hair, away from her face. I take off my coat, and lay it over her. She must be freezing. Using my teeth, I tear off a sleeve from my shirt, and use it to bind her head.

She's going to be okay. I know that.

I look up. The star is still there, but I can feel something stronger.

I look to the side of me. And there she is. An outline of her, that I knew only I will ever see.

And I realise how the sight of her, calms me.

And I realise how this feels normal.

How this feels right.

And I realise that, I will never see her again.

She's as beautiful as ever. She kneels down next to me, so we're the same height. We don't know what to say.

"You wanted to say goodbye" she whispers. "But you never needed to. I was always there".

I nod. "I know. I could feel you sometimes".

She looks like she is made of stars but her eyes. Her eyes are still as green as they have always been.

She smiles. "It was stupid of me, holding on like that. I should have gone immediately. But I loved you. I couldn't let go of you".

I look at her, my first love. "I didn't want to let go of you. I didn't want to stop loving you."

She looks deep into my eyes, like she used too.

"I understand now. You don't have too. You just have to love her".

She nods towards Seren and she smiles at her.

She stands up "Remember, Nathan… The memories never go. And the emotions remain with the memories. And the love remains. Always. I was wrong. But now I understand. There are different kinds of love. And I now know, how you can love Seren, but still love me".

I smile wistfully, and also, in a weird way, slightly happily. "

"Rissa, I could never stop loving you."

She laughs "And I thought that was a bad thing. But it's how life and love fit."

She opens her mouth, as she if wanted to say something more, but then…she frowns, and cocks her head on one side, as if she is listening for something.

Her eyes reflect our delight and incredibility.

Slowly, surely, our gaze flickers up to the night sky.

To see a silver light streak across the sky. Followed by another. And another, until I lose count.

Finally, after so long, the meteors finally came, tearing through the fabric of the world, and onto the next, carrying with them the souls of humanity.

Rissa laughs in delight, in astonishment, in amazement.

The stars seem to dance though her, though the fabric of what made her.

She gazes up the sky, with that knowing, unworldly smile, until she has taken in as much as she can.

She turns her eyes back onto me. With a gentle jolt, I see that her green eyes have become the star filled night.

We look at each other, a long gaze that says more that words and dialogue ever could.

And we know this is *it.*

I close my eyes.

When I can bring myself to open them, she's gone.

Her star remains.

I glance down at Seren.

She's wide awake, and looking straight at me.

For the first time, I see her eyes how they were intended to be. Intelligent, inquisitive and so full of vitality I have to look closely to make sure she is real.

I let my hand reach out, and take hers. She holds mine tightly.

Halting at first, but increasing in tempo, I whisper a collection of words that I have kept inside myself for so long. I started to wonder whether I would forget how to even say them.

These words are used almost on a daily basis. Everyone will say them at some point in their lives. Maybe not in this order, maybe not together. But they will be said.

They fit life and love together, like they belong. They fit individuals together. And it's how life, humanity and the insanity it brings work.

I almost thought that with these words used so much, they wouldn't be enough to describe how I really felt.

But I was wrong. They come out strong, and they come out *mine.*

We are all mad here Seren Ambern, and *I love you.*

They describe everything perfectly.

And to my immense relief, happiness, and undesirable delight, she says her words back.

Then, almost like an invisible signal, we look up at the night sky together.

And a meteor flies. Followed by another, and another.

The orb we call Earth, is surrounded.

They light up the sky.

We don't need to say another word.

(52) Clarissa.

As I leave, the stars continue to shine. Each one, a small fragment of humanity. And soon, I will join them. My atoms will split, and recycle, making something new. My soul will become part of Earth and Space. Of Everything and Anything. And I'll be at peace. I'm letting go.

And I'm flying. I'm falling strong. Nathan described me as a night sky. But for the moment, I am a meteorite. As I fly and fall, I'll break apart. I'm burning free. I'm burning out. The last of my humanity breaks free, and I can see Earth.

An orb that seems too small, too miniscule, to contain all it does.

My memories flow out. I can almost see them.

Spiralling emotions spinning and shining.

A life.

I'm part of the stars I loved so much. I'm part of the beginning and ending of life, of time.

I was Clarissa. Now I am free.

I have loved the stars too fondly to be fearful of the night....

My faith will guide me on my way amongst the stars.

Epilogue: One year later.

Daniel had once said to her, that she would achieve the impossible but Seren told me she disagrees. She believes that the things that happen to her are impossible, not what she does.

After support group, we say goodbye to Ally, and we walk slowly to the place that appears more of a park, than a place of rest.

Seren stops at the gate, and looks up at me. But I hold out my hand, and she takes it. We walk through together.

She hasn't been yet, but on the anniversary of Daniel's death, it seemed right.

The last year has been up and down, but I wouldn't regret it for one moment. Neither would Seren.

The police and an ambulance crew found us a couple of minutes later. They confirmed that we were fine, and couldn't decide whether to praise or condemn my actions. But they don't realise the entire truth about it.

It doesn't matter. We do.

Seren got better after that. She accepted it wasn't her fault. And she's learnt how to love again. And I'm so lucky, that she loves me.

Meanwhile, for me, any awkwardness or panic or guilt I might have felt faded, until I looked over my shoulder for it, and realised it wasn't there. And I've learnt how to love Seren, but also Clarissa.

It wasn't an easy road. And sometimes we went downhill. But we had each other. And we helped each other to get back uphill.

And now, Seren's ready. I lead her to the small building, where the large book is displaced. Instead of seeing a red kite, and the comet, we see a drawing of two hands clasping each other. Seren, reads the inscription quietly, and smiles to herself.

She nods to me, to show she's ready. We walk out together, to where the ashes for Daniel Luccan were spread.

And above us, the stars shine bright.

The brightest one walks with me.

I don't have much regard or patience for an old man sitting on a throne in the sky. But, I now know there is more to this life than I could ever understand.

So, I offer a quick...I don't know what to call it....to whoever may be listening.

Let the stars continue to shine, let the stars continue to explode. Let supernovas and nebulas expel elements and molecules of us around the galaxies. Let our lives be full of wonder and delight, and let them be full of confusion and mystery.

Explode like supernovas and live like one. Trace the constellations and elements back to the moment where time began. Where all of matter, and what matters, compressed into a single point, let go, and started running across the galaxy. Where elements and molecules combined and throw themselves outwards, into the unknown. When, by some miraculous chance, the crazy, chaotic, and insane thing we call life, was created.